Carissa Ann Lynch is a USA Today-bestselling author. She resides in Floyds Knobs, Indiana with her husband, children, and collection of books. She's always loved to read and never considered herself a "writer" until a few years ago when she couldn't find a book to read and decided to try writing her own story. With a background in psychology, she's always been a little obsessed with the darker areas of the mind and social problems.

carissaannlynch.wordpress.com

f facebook.com/CarissaAnnLynchauthor
🐦 twitter.com/carissaannlynch

Also by Carissa Ann Lynch

My Sister is Missing

Without a Trace

Like, Follow, Kill

The One Night Stand

Whisper Island

SHE LIED SHE DIED

CARISSA ANN LYNCH

One More Chapter
a division of HarperCollins*Publishers* Ltd
1 London Bridge Street
London SE1 9GF

1st Floor, Watermarque Building, Ringsend Road
Dublin 4, Ireland
www.harpercollins.co.uk

This paperback edition 2021
First published in Great Britain in ebook format
by HarperCollins*Publishers* 2020

A catalogue record of this book is available from the British Library

ISBN: 978-0-00-842103-8

This novel is entirely a work of fiction. The names, characters and
incidents portrayed in it are the work of the author's imagination. Any
resemblance to actual persons, living or dead, events or localities is
entirely coincidental.

Printed and bound in Great Britain by
CPI Group (UK) Ltd, Croydon CR0 4YY

"A truth that's told with bad intent
Beats all the lies you can invent."

— William Blake, "Auguries of Innocence"

Chapter One

I was nine years old when the murder happened.

Old enough to taste fresh-found fear in the air; young enough to feel unscathed by it.

Alone in the farmhouse, I squatted on my haunches in front of my brother Jack's bedroom window, eyes peeping over the ledge as far as they dared, faded binoculars shielding my face.

Jack would have killed me if he knew what I was doing because: 1. I was never allowed to enter his room, uninvited. 2. I'd gone through his trunk, which contained his "private things" (if you consider pics of naked girls with hairy bushes, and a pair of binoculars, "private") and worst of all: 3. I'd borrowed those precious binoculars.

Jack was away, visiting with our dad's aunt, my quirky Great Aunt Lane. Six years my senior, Jack and I were as close as two siblings that spread apart in age could be, I guess.

But Jack's anger and disapproval about me being in his room were the farthest thing from my mind ... he wasn't here to stop me, and even if he was ... something important was happening, something that went above and beyond everyday sibling squabbles.

I'd been quarantined to my bedroom, courtesy of Mom and Dad.

"Don't come out until we tell you."

"We have an important meeting to tend to."

But *I knew*. I didn't know *what* exactly ... but I knew something bad had happened.

Sirens raged across the field, so loud my chest rumbled, thrumming in rhythm with the abhorrent beat.

My room—my temporary prison—was equipped with two windows, but unfortunately, both faced the trees. *Wrong side.*

I'd fought hard for this room—it was slightly smaller than my brother's, but the rich green view was superior, and it had a built-in bookshelf to boot. Now, for the first time, I regretted my choice.

The urgency and excitement ... that knocking fear ... that call of *importance*—all of it was coming from the other side of the house.

So, I'd crawled across the knotty pine floors, army-woman style, until I'd reached my brother's bedroom. It was unlocked, as was his precious trunk, and the binoculars were the prize I'd been hoping for.

I adjusted the binoculars on my face. They were old, too big for me. But they were my best bet because the chaos was happening across the field.

Through the foggy lens, I searched for my mother and father. But they were nowhere to be found.

There were others—several *others*, in fact. A cluster of people formed a strange, mystic circle in the centre of the field, a cloud of low-slung fog forming a blanket around them. Like ancient druids, they were engaged in some sort of ritual…

I let my wild imagination run its course, then I readjusted my viewpoint.

The source of the sirens was obvious—an ambulance had pulled right through the center of Daddy's field, mowing down crops and kicking up mud. There were thick wet tire tracks in the soil.

The doors of the ambulance were left flung open on the driver's side and cab; the flash of the sirens glittered like rubies.

The circle-jerks weren't moving, but I could tell they were *looking. Looking at what, exactly?* I wondered. Heads ducked low, hands on hips … there was one man with his hands folded behind his head. Another was a woman covering her mouth and nose…

My next thought—*a stupid one*—was that maybe there was one of those crop circles in Daddy's field. I'd read something about them in Jack's sci-fi magazine, the one with the grainy image of Nessie, with her long neck and protruding humps, on the cover. I hadn't believed a word of it.

As I trained the binoculars on the circle, willing the lens to focus, I realized that most of them were in uniform. *Cops. Boring!*

Suddenly, the man with his hands behind his head pivoted. He turned away from the others. Moving, *marching,* he was headed straight toward my house.

No, not the house ... toward Mom and Dad. For the first time, I spotted them, huddled at the edge of the property. My dad, William, and my mother, Sophie. They looked too soft and young to be farmers. And, in reality, they weren't. Just two young people trying to have a place to call their own, to carry on a family tradition...

For the first time, they looked their age, faces grim and tight with worry.

Dad's hairy arm was draped over Mom's tiny, narrow shoulders. She was ... *shaking.*

As the mysterious policeman crossed the field, trotting toward them, I was mesmerized by him ... with his thick black hair and chiseled body, he looked scruffy and world-weary, but in a good way—like that actor in *Hollywood Detective.*

He stopped in front of Mom and Dad, hands resting on his waistband, fingers itching his gun like an outlaw from the Wild West.

4

Suddenly, he pointed across the field, gesturing wildly. Even behind a sheet of glass, I thought I heard Mom's sorrowful wail, "Oh noooo."

There was a gap in the circle now, I realized, pulling my eyes away from the cop and my parents. I zoomed in as far as the binoculars allowed, and for the first time, I could see inside the secret circle.

I could see what the fuss was about.

Knuckles white, I willed my hands not to shake. Willed myself not to look away...

There was a girl in the center of the circle. Fragile and small, she lay curled up on the ground, like one of those pill bugs we called "rollie pollies".

It wasn't natural, the way she was bent ... arms and legs sharply curved and folded in, like a clay sculpture you could shape and mold, bend at will...

Could it be an alien ... or better yet ... a mannequin posed for a prank?

Sitting back on my haunches, I took a few deep breaths, then poked my head up again.

This time, the crowd had thinned out more, and as I zoomed in again ... I saw her completely. For the first time, the lenses were crystal clear.

She was real—*human*. White skin, pale hair to match. Thin, white strands of hair blew around her face like corn silk. Her fingers were curled up by her mouth, nails painted matte black like the night sky.

Eyelids open, one gray eye bulged out at me like a grape

5

being squeezed between my thumb and forefinger …

The rolling in my stomach was less of a roll and more of a lurch. I was barely on my feet when the vomit came. It sprang from my mouth and nose, and although I tried, pathetically, to catch it in my hands, there was just too much of it.

I puked on my brother's favorite *Star Wars* blanket and CD tower, then I curled up on the floor like that *thing* in the field, trying to erase the image burned on the back of my eyelids.

It's not real. It's not real. Please tell me it's not real.

Chapter Two

T hree truths.
   One lie.

I've lived in the same shitty town for most of my life.

A girl named Jenny Juliott was murdered in my own "backyard".

I'm an aspiring writer who moonlights as a Kmart cashier.

Jenny Juliott's killer was never caught.

———————

That original image of Jenny's face—moon-white and ominous in the early morning light—those bulgy eyeballs and dead gray irises ... *that* image had evolved over the years. Replaced by one replica after another ... *there is her face, the way I think I saw it that day ... and then there are the memories, and later, the flashes of crime scene photos I pored over in my free time.*

I didn't know her—of course I didn't; she was fourteen and I was nine. We may have lived in the same shitty town of Austin, Indiana, but we didn't know each other at all. Despite what they say about small towns, we do *not* all know each other.

But, over the years, I came to know everything about the girl with the white-blonde hair and the haunting gray eyes who smoked skinny cigarettes called Virginia Slims and who would never age a day over fourteen in the hearts and minds of Austin's residents.

Jenny Juliott had a mother, a father, and an older brother around Jack's age.

It was weeks before the crime scene was cleared from our property, reflective yellow caution tape stirring in the wind like a warning flag. Little bits of it floating around the property like confetti...

Years later, after the crime was solved and her killer was locked away in prison, I was digging around, looking for dandelions—not the yellow ones, but the ones you wish on —and I found what looked like a strip of gold in the dirt.

But it wasn't gold; far from it. It was that stupid old crime scene tape, bits of it still rotting around the edges of our property, still strung up in the branches of trees where it had gotten blown around that summer. *A reminder that it wasn't all a bad dream, as much as we wanted it to be...*

After Jenny was murdered, my parents pretended

nothing happened … this was their way. That had *always* been their way. Perhaps they saw it as protecting me, but I saw it as treating me like an imbecile.

The lies we sometimes tell ourselves—or, in their case, lies were simply omissions.

"Nothing for you to worry about, dear."

"She was a wild girl, must have got caught up in some trouble."

"This is the safest town in three counties."

Lies.

Lies.

Lies.

Because the first thing my parents did was replace the locks on the front, back, and sides of the house. Days of riding my bike to my best friend Adrianna's were over. So were the days of slumber parties, playing outside alone, and walking to school or down to the park with friends.

Most of my friends, and their parents too, were too afraid to come to the farm. As though my family might be involved in her death, or that death itself might be contagious if you got too close.

There are two types of people in this world: those who drive by fast, avoiding the scene of a tragedy, and those who slow to a crawl, chicken heads bobbing up and down through the windows just to catch a glimpse of where a young girl died.

After the tragedy on the farm, we got a little of both

types. Those who wanted to avoid us, and the creeps who wouldn't leave us alone.

At school, there were stirrings … I heard a few things, but since I was only in third grade at the time, a lot of the true grisly details were shielded from us.

But it didn't stop us from creating our own.

"Someone killed her. Hacked her up with a chainsaw. She must have pissed someone off right good."

"I heard aliens abducted her then dropped her down from the sky."

"They fed her to the pigs on the Breyas farm."

"Oink oink, Natalie. Oink oink."

Lies. All lies.

We didn't even own pigs, dammit.

It wasn't until I turned the ripe age of fourteen, the same age Jenny was when she died, that I learned some things that *were* true.

Jenny Juliott wasn't killed on my family's farm—she was dumped there. She had been strangled and stabbed, and the police knew who did it, because the killer confessed: the confessor's name was Chrissy Cornwall.

Chrissy Cornwall: resident Austin tough girl who grew up on the "other side of the tracks". It just so happened that that "other side" was across the creek and through the woods from my family's farm.

Chrissy was fifteen when she committed the murder. She had jet-black hair, oddly streaked with flakes of gray at an early age—or was it white, like lightning? I couldn't be certain. I knew her even less than I knew Jenny.

Chrissy and Jenny were not friends; they didn't even attend the same school.

Chrissy was "homeschooled" by her mother—and by "homeschooled", I mean that they requested to teach her at home but never did. Unlike Jenny, who grew up in a nice middle-class home with a stay-at-home mother and a pastor father and attended Austin Middle School with most of the other kids in town, Chrissy was an outcast. An unknown.

Jenny bought ripped jeans from outlet malls and painted her nails black with twelve-dollar polish. Chrissy's pants were ripped with time, and from scrapping with her hoodlum brothers on the front lawn of her daddy's trailer lot.

Jenny was smart, pretty. Chrissy was … I don't know what you'd call her. Poor white trash, I guess.

On paper, Jenny and Chrissy had nothing in common. But there was one thread that tied them together, and that thread had a name: John Bishop.

John went to school with Jenny and the others, and he and Jenny were dating. But, unbeknownst to Jenny and the rest of the kids, John had a girl on the side—the dirty girl whose parents didn't send her to school, the girl with the strange black-gray hair who lived in a trailer.

And that trailer was a hop and a skip from my family's farm.

There were many people to blame for Chrissy's actions

—her parents for their lack of supervision and education, the state for not following up on reports of abuse, the school for letting a girl who didn't attend there kidnap another in the school parking lot …

But most of all, we blamed the guilty party: Chrissy herself.

She was jealous and angry, and determined to make Jenny pay for messing around with John, whom she felt she had a claim to.

Those are the scarecrow details.

Over the years, much more has come out. But some parts are still a mystery. I guess when it comes down to it … you can never fully understand the heart of a person—why would anyone *kill* someone over a stupid boy? And to do it so brutally…

I hadn't thought about the case in over a decade. Chrissy had been tried and convicted, sentenced to life in prison despite her age at the time of the crime. I used to be obsessed, but not any more.

The media had forgotten, as had I; we'd moved on to similar cases, ones with gorier details and more exciting bylines splashed across the nightly news.

But, of course, Austin hadn't forgotten. And as much as I tried to push it away, I hadn't let it go either. Jenny was always there; a memory, a warning … a piece of my childhood I couldn't get back. Perhaps there was a small part of me that blamed her death for the fallout of my own childhood…

A lot can change in thirty years—but a lot can stay the same.

The third step on the corkscrew staircase still creaks when I step on it; the bathroom and cellar still stink of Clorox and mold like they did when Mom and Dad lived here.

Inheriting my family's farm ten years ago should have been a blessing, and when I was thirty, it had sort of felt like one. But thirty turned into thirty-five, and just last week, I celebrated my fortieth birthday the way I did my thirty-ninth—alone.

Wearing only socks and undies, I tiptoed from my room—my parents' former bedroom—and made my way for the stairs. Every light in the house was off, which was how I liked it. *If I can't see the shadows, then they can't see me…*

As I wound my way up the stairs, I caught a glimpse of moonlight through the picture windows in the kitchen … *it can't be much later than two, maybe three, in the morning…*

So, what woke me?

There were sounds, but nothing unusual. The creaky old floorboards, the low hum of the refrigerator downstairs, the soft ticking of the grandfather clock in my office, which I'd converted from Jack's old bedroom.

Sometimes I caught glimpses of the place as it was before … Mom in the living room reading paperback mysteries, Dad at the table with the *Times*, and Jack mounted up in the living room watching *Star Wars* … their ghosts, just a flicker of movement, a light hollowed sound through the walls…

But there was something else this morning, something *real* … whiny and synchronous, coming from the side of the house. And just like that, my legs were shorter and thinner … I was nine years old again, creeping toward my brother's bedroom window, following the warning moans that lay beyond the dingy clapboard walls of my daddy's farmhouse.

It can't be. There's no reason for an ambulance … no way there's anything out there. Maybe this is all a dream … a memory…

The door to Jack's old bedroom was closed up tight. I'd like to think I kept it closed to ensure the privacy of my home office, but in truth, I think I did it out of habit.

Jack would want it that way.

I nudged the door open with my foot and, trancelike, I tiptoed toward the window facing the field.

When someone dies, it's not unusual for their family or friends to keep their rooms exactly as they once were. But with Jack … I couldn't. Erasing him felt better, easier … and so, the first thing I did when I moved back home ten years ago was tear out the carpet and take his old bedroom furniture out and replace it with a modern oak desk and shelves. A computer and a desk—the necessities for any writer. But I hadn't written a word in years.

As I edged closer to the window, there was no doubt: someone was out in the field. But that sound … it wasn't sirens; no gaudy red rubies bouncing through the trees, ricocheting from my heart to my head.

But what I saw took my breath away.

A circle of people, each one holding a candle in front of them.

Thirty years later, and still: the first thing that comes to mind is a pagan ritual.

They were singing, something low and melancholy, flames from their candles casting ghoulish shadows over their faces.

I felt a flicker of rage. *How dare they waltz on my property like they own the place? This isn't a tourist attraction!*

But in a way it had been ... people had come from all over to see the "spot" the first few years after the murder. Sometimes, Dad would chase them off with a shotgun ... but after a while, he took to ignoring them. *"Easier that way,"* he told me.

But since I'd come home, there hadn't been a single unwanted visitor. *Until now.*

I'd assumed that most had forgotten Jenny Juliott and the girl who'd killed her.

Snapping the bolts to unlock the window, I shoved on the glass and poked my head all the way out, forgetting about my lacy black bra.

"Hey! What are you doing?" I shouted. It was windy, and chilly for October, and my words blew back angrily in my face.

I tried again. "Hello! It's, like, two in the morning..." I

screamed so loud I could feel veins protruding from my forehead.

And just like that, the singing stopped. Nearly a dozen heads turned my way.

"Hey, Natalie," came a woman's voice in the dark. As I squinted, she stepped into the sliver of moonlight in the field and pushed back the hood of a dark gray sweatshirt.

She looked familiar, but I couldn't place her. *Was she someone I went to school with?*

It's funny how over time every face looks familiar, but at the same time, I could never remember names. My childhood just a splotch on my memory board...

"Hey," I answered, dully.

Another woman stepped up beside the first. This one had black curls and, despite the chill in the air, she was wearing a white T-shirt and thin multi-colored yoga pants. A face I'd never forget: Adrianna Montgomery, forgotten friend turned local columnist. I tried to avoid her in town at all costs, but I saw her occasionally at the supermarket and Kmart when I was working. I usually pretended not to and luckily, she did the same.

"Natalie, it's good to see you. Sorry we're out here, but we tried to call you first ... we wanted to honor Jenny, especially considering the latest news. We can't forget what that monster did to her, you know?" Adrianna said.

The latest news?

My lousy paychecks from Kmart weren't enough to justify getting cable. I had just enough to eat, fill up my car with gas, and gas the tractor for cutting the field in the warmer months ... I didn't keep up with local news, or national news either.

"What news? I haven't seen it," I said, voice barely above a whisper.

The other faces in the crowd slowly materialized like old ghosts; I recognized a few of my former classmates and Jenny's brother in the crowd. My heart sank with guilt when I saw him. Although I'd seen most of the others around town, I hadn't seen him in years. I'd heard that he moved away.

As a kid, whenever Mom or I would see Jenny's family in town after the murder, we'd avert our eyes. Try to make ourselves invisible. Not because we blamed them, of course, but because we didn't know what to say ... *what can you say to someone who's lost a loved one that way?* And perhaps, there was also a nasty little sliver inside us, that selfish part that worried their tragedy might become ours. That somehow it was contagious ... in the same way people avoided me and my home because of what happened here...

Unfortunately for us, avoiding the Juliotts didn't do us any good because look at what happened to Jack.

So, as Mike Juliott stepped forward, I forced myself to meet his gaze. He was her brother—if anyone had a right to be here it was him.

Mike cleared his throat. "Didn't you hear? They're letting that monster out. Bitch got paroled. Chrissy Cornwall is coming home."

Chapter Three

C*hrissy Cornwall is coming home.* Five words I thought I'd never hear.

Mike Juliott's mid-morning announcement rolled over and back in my gullet as I scraped watery eggs onto my plate and buttered two pieces of toast.

It was Thursday, which meant I had the day off (a pretty shitty day to have off, I admit), but I was up early anyway.

No matter how late my mother stayed up at night, she always rose for the day by 5am. As a kid, her early-morning antics had irritated me no end—on weekends, I'd tried to sleep in, but then I'd hear her: banging pots in the kitchen, boiling tea by the light of the moon.

One time I asked her why she did it—*what is the point of it all?*

"I used to sleep in like you do, but then I realized that I feel

better about myself when I wake up early. There's no guilt, and it makes for a good night's rest."

At the time, it sounded stupid.

But as an adult, I understood.

There is nothing worse than lying in bed at night with regrets and getting up early to accomplish everything I need to do reduces that slightly.

I munched my toast, ate a spoonful of eggs, then chugged half a cup of coffee. There was a list of things I needed to do—grocery shopping, laundry, etc.

But all I could think about was Chrissy Cornwall.

Could it be true?

When they sentenced her to life, we all assumed that meant she would stay in prison for "life".

I understood why Mike was angry; he had every right to be. And the other people ... well, most of the townsfolk had children, and I could understand why they didn't want a murderer in town.

But my heart was in knots about it, my feelings mixed. Chrissy was fifteen when she got locked up. *That must make her, what? Forty-five or forty-six?*

Thinking back to who I was at fifteen versus who I was now ... so many things had changed.

But at the same time, nothing has.

I was still the same girl deep inside, only now my mousy brown hair was streaked with gray, my face a spider web of wrinkles and broken blood vessels.

And as I looked around the same dingy kitchen from my

childhood, with its peeling daisy wallpaper and cock-a-doodle-doo plaques on the wall … I felt more certain than ever that time was standing still.

I'm still here. Still me. I never thought I would be stuck in the same place, but I am. And if I haven't changed much, has Chrissy? Do any of us … really?

I left as soon as I had the chance, right after my high school graduation. I had big dreams of going to college and becoming a writer, and I fulfilled one of those—I worked a tough package-handling job that helped pay for my tiny apartment and covered the school expenses that my student loans didn't. I sacrificed my social life and moved to a college town in neighboring Kentucky where I had no family, no friends… I thought I'd have plenty of time for the fun stuff after college. But then Jack happened and somehow, I was back where I started—doing nothing with my degree, and just as lonely (if not more) here than I ever had been.

Yes, I had changed. It was hard not to after all that I'd gone through. And for the sake of Austin, I hoped Chrissy had changed too.

If she was really coming home, the town would be buzzing with it soon.

They already are, I realized, circling back to those ghoulish faces I'd seen in the field last night.

I scrubbed my dish and fork with soap and water, then left them to dry in the sink. Taking my coffee with me, I trudged up the stairs to my office. It had been so long since

I'd turned on my computer, since I'd felt the punchy feel of my keys.

I missed writing. But mostly, I missed the hope I'd held onto for so long—that one day I'd produce a great book. I wrote every night in my little apartment in Kentucky, mostly fiction—in the small gaps of time between work and school. I'd tried pitching some of my ideas to small publishers and agents, but without any luck.

Since coming home ten years ago, I'd been unable to write much of anything. Austin was, essentially, uninspiring.

My fingers glided effortlessly across the keyboard, typing Chrissy's name in the Google search bar. I shivered despite the heat of my coffee—*is the furnace going out? Why is it so damn cold in October?*

It had been years since I'd checked up on Chrissy or researched the Juliott murder. As a teen and young adult, I'd been obsessed, and the invention of the internet had been both a blessing and a curse—it provided a wider window for my obsession and provided access to the horrors I'd tried—and failed—to forget.

The crime scene photos online were eerie. Some fake, but most of them real. And like the photos, the stories were a mix—conspiracy theories, repetitive summaries of the case. Podcasts and articles were helpful, and addictive, but the story was too complex for a six-paragraph op-ed.

It's not like the story hadn't been written—it had: *twice*. *Little Angel in the Field* and *Evil in Austin* had flown off the shelves. I'd dreamed of writing the story myself—*who better than me?*—but I'd never been able to get past the first few pages. After all, everything had already been written… *What more do I have to add to the discussion? And what do I really know about writing true crime?*

Several news articles filled my screen: the headline *Child Killer Released* caught my eye immediately.

Child Killer Released. It wasn't a lie exactly—but it was a double entendre. Yes, Chrissy had murdered a kid—but what the headline failed to capture was the fact that she had been a kid herself when she did it. Did the person writing this intend for the reader to feel confused? Is Chrissy a child killer, or a child who killed? *She's both*, I reminded myself. *Both*.

I scrolled and scrolled, reading more: *Jenny Juliott's Killer Released from Indiana Women's Prison*. I focused on another article instead, one with a more gripping headline: *Something Wicked This Way Comes: The Monster Returns to Austin*.

I clicked, immediately recognizing the article's author, Adrianna Montgomery: class president, town know-it-all, and senior columnist of the *Austin Gazette*.

She'd been standing in the dark amongst the others last night, her eyes judging me as they had for years…

Once upon a time, we had been best of friends. But that all changed after Jenny. Adrianna's parents had fallen into the category of people who tried to avoid our family and our house as much as possible. Adrianna was no longer allowed to come over, and at school, she avoided me there too. Even now, when I saw her in town, there was this wall between us ... something dark and hard. *Impenetrable.* I hated her for turning her back on me, for standing back while the others at school teased me about the farm and what happened there. And now, seeing her flourishing as a journalist made me cringe with jealousy.

I read the first few lines of her article:

It's been thirty years since the beloved Jenny Juliott was brutally sacrificed on the Breyas Farm. It feels like only yesterday to those who loved her. So, imagine the shock and outrage we all felt when we heard the news: Chrissy Cornwall is getting out of prison. What sort of failing system lets a monster like her out after only thirty years? Townspeople should take to the streets, petition the mayor—

I minimized the screen, rubbing my eyes in annoyance. The article was bullshit. Adrianna Montgomery had been my age when the murder happened. She didn't know the *beloved* Jenny any more than I did. And calling her murder a 'sacrifice' made it sound like something from the occult. The murder didn't even happen on our property ... she was *dumped* here.

Any minute now, the field will be crawling with reporters ... hunting witches in Austin. Thanks a lot, Adrianna.

I clicked on another article, this one national news from

Crime Times. I waited for the grainy image to load, tapping the desk impatiently.

When it did, I gasped.

It was a split shot—on the left, a mugshot of Chrissy with her jet-black hair and hypnotic blue eyes. I'd seen this photo a million times over the years—she had grinned in her arrest photo, exposing gapped front teeth and her feral demeanor. Little shocks of white in her hair gave her an ethereal quality.

She looked like a maniac.

But the photo on the right was something else entirely … it showed a middle-aged woman, with stringy salt-and-pepper hair and sad gunmetal-gray eyes being escorted out of prison. This time, when Chrissy's eyes met the camera, she hadn't smiled.

She looked downright sad and ashamed. Defeated.

I maximized the image, studying the woman that I hadn't seen in years—there had been a few photos from prison, but nothing in more than a decade. Supposedly, she had denied all interviews with the press after her trial.

There were no traces of the girl in the woman. *Where did she go?*

Her jowls were thicker, her chin whiskery … and she'd put on nearly fifty pounds. It was hard to correlate the wild teen in the mug shot with this sad old woman beside her.

Skipping over the article itself, I typed in the search bar: Where is Chrissy Cornwall moving to in Austin.

I didn't expect to find an answer—surely, she'd try to keep her address private. And I knew she wasn't moving back to her childhood home by the creek because it had been abandoned for years now, her deadbeat parents skipping town for good and local teens trashing the place during midnight drunk dares to visit the murderer's house...

But my search provided an immediate hit. Not only was her address online, but also the addresses for every living relative of hers in the country.

Someone had discovered her location, essentially doxing her.

4840 Willow Run Road.

Stunned, I settled back in my chair, reading the address over and over again. Not only was Chrissy coming home, but she was moving less than a mile from here. It made sense why she'd picked it; Austin was a small farming community, but most people lived in the center business district of town. She was moving to the outskirts near me—the place where outcasts reside.

Is she already there? Already moved in? I wondered. The thought of her being so close, breathing the same recycled air as me, made my stomach twist with unease.

I did another search, trying to figure out when she had been released exactly. I got an instant hit—*they let her out two days ago.*

Willow Run Road was a long road, but I guessed she was moving into one of the trailers people sold or rented out there. *Who is paying for her place?* I wondered. *Somebody must be.*

With a sideways glance out the window, I looked on as reporters grazed through my field like wide-eyed cows.

I didn't even hear them pull in.

A flash of cold white skin, those bulgy gray eyes…

I stood up and went to the window, lowering the blinds.

The monster is back.

But is she a monster … or simply misunderstood? What truly motivated her crime that day? My thoughts were stuck on those two words: *child killer.*

Even now, a small part of me was filled with doubt. The violence of it … it didn't seem like something a kid would do. It had never made sense to me.

Most of the conspiracy theories I'd read online were bogus—there were people who believed she was framed, some blaming her parents, Jenny's brother … even a few who mentioned my brother or parents.

But her guilt was never in question. After all, she confessed to the crime.

And yet, I'd always felt like there was something more … a missing link to the story. Something more than a silly crush on a boy had to have motivated such violence…

The media had lost interest in the case over the years, but I had a feeling with her recent release, the cycle would begin again.

If I'm going to write the story, now is the time.

But what is there to say that hasn't already been hashed over a million times? The only person who can tell me more is Chrissy herself.

Determinedly, I took a seat in front of the computer and pulled up Microsoft Word. I started typing a letter, but then, changing my mind, I opened a drawer, taking out thick tan sheets of stationery and a ballpoint pen.

Handwritten is more personal.

Head bent low, I began crafting a letter to a killer.

The chances of Chrissy Cornwall agreeing to speak with me were slim to none, but what did I have to lose?

So, imagine my surprise when, a few days later, she showed up at my front door.

Chapter Four

I cy cold breaths crackled the morning air and I shivered, clutching the thick gray quilt to my chest. *That damn furnace ... it has to be like, what? Fifty degrees in here?*

My shift didn't start until noon and after my late-night scrolling on subreddit about the case, I needed an extra hour or two of sleep...

I closed my eyes, teeth chattering despite the heavy blanket.

My eyes fluttered open again as I heard the panic-inducing thumps at the front door. Even now, thirty years later, the sounds of knocking disturbed me. Reporters, cops ... you never knew who would turn up at the Breyas farm.

Ignore them.

I scurried deeper under the blankets, covering my mouth and nose. Squeezing my eyes shut as I tried to keep my nerves at bay...

But the thumping grew louder. More determined.

Fuck.

And there was something else too … the buzz and whine of voices. I pushed the covers back, listening.

There's more than one person out there.

The whir of voices grew louder, until there was no mistaking it: people were shouting.

I threw the covers off with a low growl and stumbled out of my parents' old bed.

The wood floors felt like patches of ice beneath my bare feet as I tiptoed to the front living room, trying not to make a sound.

"What are your plans here? How do you know Natalie Breyas?" A nervous rush of fear at the sound of my own name lodged in my chest and throat. Breathlessly, I pressed my ear to the thick wooden door, struggling to interpret the buzz of what could only be an angry hive of reporters outside.

A sick trickle of fear came over me as I had a flash of memory—my dad in the doorway, cameras flashing in his eyes … he'd reached for one of the cameras, hands tangling with the reporter instead, and as I'd watched the incident unfold on the local news, I'd been filled with horror and shame. My dad's reaction to the reporters had been understandable, but not to them … *Is Robert Breyas a violent man? What does he have to hide?* That's what the next day's headlines had read.

They had wanted to make him look bad. And they succeeded.

They also succeeded in driving my mother away. She was never the same after that, and finally she left us for good, at a time in my life when I needed her most.

I yelped as another bang vibrated through my cheek and ricocheted through my skull.

Whoever was on the other side wasn't giving up.

Remembering my dad's regrettable fury, I composed myself, smoothing licks of wild hair from my face and wiping residue from last night's mascara from my cheeks.

"Evil bitch!" That was a man's voice, a booming rasp of pure hatred.

Before I could change my mind, I unlatched the deadbolt and swung the front door open. Morning sunlight and the flash of a dozen cameras bombarded me, and temporarily, I was blind. Shielding my face, I squinted out at the hazy crowds of people and the mess of news vans tearing up my front yard.

But they all faded to static … background noise … because leaning against the side of my house, head ducked protectively to her chest, was someone I recognized. In the dusty haze of cold morning light, she looked almost … *celestial*. Head lifted, her eyes raising to meet mine…

She opened her mouth and said, "Hello. I'm Chrissy Cornwall."

Chapter Five

As though I didn't already know that. How could I not? I'd studied her face ... dreamed of it, even.

Once again, I was baffled by her appearance. On TV a few days ago, she had looked old and pitiful. Some might even say *regretful*.

But now, face red and rageful, jaw jumping in her cheek ... she looked like the feral woman from before.

"Who the fuck do they think they are, huh? I did my time. And I'm still doing it! They surround Dennis's trailer night and day, banging on the window like vultures. That has to be a crime, doesn't it? Harassment, or something?!"

I couldn't respond. Couldn't *breathe*.

Chrissy Cornwall, convicted child killer and killer of children, was standing in the center of my living room, hands on her hips like she owned the place. Unknowingly, I had backed myself into a corner of the room, arms crossed over my chest and backside pressed against a wobbly bookshelf that housed dozens of true crime novels. *Including the two that featured none other than Chrissy herself.*

Chrissy was tall and broad-shouldered—larger than she'd looked in her photos. She unraveled a soft blue scarf from around her neck, endlessly twisting, then plucked a matching wool hat off her head. I watched as she shook out her shiny long locks of hair—it had been washed recently, the scent of jasmine floating through the air. Her hair had also been dyed—the wiry black hair with the silvery streaks was gone, replaced with an odd attempt at going blonde that gave her hair a peachy look.

Chrissy raised her still-dark eyebrows at me and smiled expectantly. When I said nothing, she sighed, then folded up her scarf. She placed it neatly on the loveseat, along with her hat.

"I got your letter. I thought you wanted to talk to me," she said, her eyes crinkling with amusement. She leaned her head right, then left, studying me, then added, "You look scared. Don't be scared of me."

A small whoosh of breath escaped from between my lips. *As though being told, "Don't be scared of me" by a convicted killer was any real consolation.*

Truth was, I wasn't so much scared as I was *shocked.* My brain running twenty paces behind, I couldn't catch up with what my eyes were seeing.

Like when I'd found Jack… I'd been … *frozen.* Brain too stunned to absorb the truth, too slow to react.

I cleared my throat. "Ummm ... would you like to sit down?" It was someone else's voice coming out of me, robotic and strange.

"Yes, but can we move away from here?" Chrissy thumbed the front window behind her. The curtains were drawn—they always were—but there were still people outside. Talking. Shouting. Then another bang at the front door.

But that was all background noise. My mind sharpened as I studied Chrissy's face. *I sent her a letter and she came. She actually came to my house...*

Her face was tired ... and haggard. A web of wrinkles sprouted from her eyes and mouth, and a scar I hadn't noticed in her picture the other day—a shimmery white line on her left cheek—ran from the bottom of her left eye to the top of her lip line. *Did someone cut her in prison?*

I'd asked if I could write her story. But I didn't ask her to show up like this. It seems like a violation—turning up at my front door with no warning, the rabid press trailing behind her ... but this is what I wanted, isn't it?

I thought back to my letter ... to me, neatly folding the paper and sliding it in the envelope ... to me, slowly and hopefully licking the seal, and carefully filling out the return address when I could have simply left it blank.

You knew what you were doing when you sent it, I told myself. *And it's not like she couldn't have found out where you lived anyway ... a few simple clicks online and we're all exposed these days.*

This was my chance—the one I'd dreamed of for so many years. Access to the story that could change my life. And a chance to hear the truth from her.

But I had to get things off on the right foot … I had to stay professional, in control.

Chrissy was staring, eyes wide and still slightly amused, as she waited for me to move, to react…

"Stay here while I change and brush my teeth. We'll talk upstairs in my office, if that works for you. Would you like some coffee or tea?"

Chrissy smiled, that sliver of amusement replaced with genuine gratitude. "Yes, please. I'm so out of breath from dealing with those fuckers outside. They followed me the whole way here, from my trailer to your house…"

My heart was drumming in my chest as I made my way through the galley kitchen and down the hall to my room to get changed. She hadn't even told me which she wanted, coffee or tea, and I had no questions prepared … no clue where to start. *And what should I do about the people on my front lawn?*

But I needn't have worried about that—I'd barely slipped into my sweater and leggings when I heard a rush of voices and then Chrissy's words shouting: "Natalie Breyas is writing my story! The true story about what happened all those years ago. So, if you want to hear what I have to say, then you'll have to wait to read the book."

I opened the door to my bedroom, smoothing my hair, body tight with shock all over again. Emerging in the hallway, I saw Chrissy towering in the open front doorway, a flash of reporters splayed before her, like lovesick—or hatesick—fans groveling to get onstage.

A roar of questions erupted, but Chrissy simply raised both arms like Jesus and shouted, "The story of my innocence is coming!"

Chapter Six

"I must admit. I'm pretty shocked you showed up at my house. What made you decide to talk to me?" I asked, a mixed flutter of anxiety and excitement building inside me.

Chrissy Cornwall sat across from me, the cherry oak desktop creating a barrier between us.

"Honestly? Your letter touched me. It didn't seem judgmental or angry. More like ... I don't know ... curious. I've wanted to tell my side of the story for a long time now. And I had a feeling you'd contact me one of these days ... I wasn't expecting it to be so soon though." Chrissy twisted her shiny peach hair in a knot at the base of her skull, fidgeting in her seat.

"Why did you expect me to reach out?" I asked, breathlessly. We didn't know each other; we'd barely crossed paths at all as children. I hadn't reached out to her over the years ... but why did it feel so *right* that she knew? *Almost like I've always expected this moment too.*

Chrissy shrugged. "I don't know. Because it happened here. You were a witness to the fallout, I suppose. More so than any of those assholes outside."

An odd sense of pride washed over me; I was glad she trusted me enough to talk, after all these years.

"Truth is, nothing about this case has ever sat well with me. It rocked my whole childhood ... my entire family, actually..." I admitted.

Chrissy nodded sympathetically, as though she understood what it felt like to be in my shoes. *But she doesn't,* I tried to remind myself. *She wasn't around to see the fallout the murder left behind; how the town went to shit, and my mother ran off and left me.*

"You are the first person from this town who has expressed interest in hearing my side of the story. And the trial ... if you followed it, then you know I didn't take the stand in my own defense. The version the lawyers gave ... well, that was their version of events. By the way, I remember your brother. How is he?"

My breath lodged in my throat at the mention of Jack. Her question had thrown me.

How is he?

Doesn't Chrissy know what happened? She's been in prison, but I know they have TVs in there ... surely, she knows the truth about Jack ...

"He passed away several years ago. I didn't realize you knew each other, much. Although I'm not surprised since you all were around the same age." I swallowed.

I waited for what I knew would come next: *I'm sorry for your loss. How did he die?* Because let's face it: when somebody young dies prematurely, we all want to know what happened. And we're all sorry. *So damn sorry.*

But Chrissy surprised me by not pushing it further.

"I met him a few times when I went to parties with my brother and with John," she explained.

The mention of John Bishop also gave me a start. He was the reason Chrissy had killed Jenny—the beginning of the end of everything for both girls. One went to prison for life and the other lost her life ... all over a boy.

But, as it turns out, "life in prison" didn't mean forever. Not in Chrissy's case.

"Are you okay? You look pale." Chrissy raised her eyebrows. I was still unnerved by her presence here; and those odd dark brows and the new hair color threw me off.

"May I be frank with you?" I asked.

Honesty. Frankness. Does Chrissy Cornwall understand those concepts, or is she as evil as the media portrayed? I wondered.

Being truthful was risky, but establishing rapport was imperative.

"Yes, please. I've always respected people who are forthright. Better that way 'cause then I always know where I stand…" Chrissy leaned forward, placing both hands on the desk. After a few seconds, I couldn't shake the feeling that this was something normal—a conversation between two girl friends over tea.

I said, "I'm completely unprepared for this. And it's important for you to know that I've never been published before. I don't have an agent or book deal lined up. I'm sure there are other people with more experience and support who could write this book about you. Don't get me wrong, I want to do it. But I need to be honest. And I'll need more time to prepare questions and talk to you, and think this through before I start..."

Chrissy waved her hands, lips puckered up in disgust. "I don't care about money or deals. I just want to tell my side of things for once. And it's okay if you're not ready. I did kind of show up on your doorstep out of the blue ... sorry about that."

I nodded. "That's okay. But coming here ... isn't it strange for you?"

Slowly, I pointed toward the office window, the one facing the field. The blinds were drawn tight, but still ... thirty years later, and the gruesome image of Jenny's corpse lying in the field hadn't faded. *Not for me.*

Chrissy glanced toward the window. Thoughtfully, she chewed on her lower lip. It was almost like she'd forgotten ... that she didn't realize she was sitting less than a football field's distance from where poor little Jenny had lain...

"Sometimes when I look out there, it's like I still expect to see her ... her body ... well, I guess you know," I said.

Nervously, I averted my eyes from hers, softly reaching over to brush my fingertips on a silver letter opener. If she had wanted to, Chrissy could have snatched it up and slit my throat the moment we entered this room. For the first time, reality set in … *I'm alone in my house with a killer. Sure, there's news media outside, but no one is here to save me.*

Daddy had owned several rifles and pistols, but I didn't have them anymore. Not after what happened with Jack…

But for some strange reason, I didn't feel afraid. Chrissy seemed genuine and … non-threatening.

Chrissy's eyes moved from the window, down to the opener I was touching, then back up at me. For a moment, I was convinced that she could read my thoughts, fears reading out like a teleprompter in front of my face…

"It must have been hard for you, growing up here after what happened."

"It was strange, to say the least," I replied.

"And your folks are the ones who found the body, right? I mean … I know they are because I read through the police notes a million times and I saw both of them at the trial. Was that stressful for you?" Chrissy asked.

Why does it feel like I'm the one being interviewed, all of a sudden?

"Yeah. I was nine at the time. My parents actually tried to keep me locked away in my room while the police investigated. But I saw the body … I saw Jenny that day."

"Jenny…" Chrissy said, her eyes watery and distant.

Her eyes glazed over; it was like she was seeing

something beyond my vision. I waited for her to elaborate, but she didn't.

Does she feel remorseful? Is she thinking about the poor girl she supposedly killed that day?

But my thoughts circled back to that speech she'd made to the reporters…

"What you said earlier about being innocent … is that true?"

Chrissy's focus was back, her eyes zeroed in on mine like two tiny black beads. For a flicker of a second, I thought I saw fury behind them.

"That's why I said yes to your letter. Why I'm saying yes to you now … because if anyone knows the details of this case and knows the story … it's you. If I can convince you of my innocence, then maybe I can convince the world. And I feel like you deserve to hear it after all these years, considering you were around to experience it at the time."

I didn't expect this interview to happen and I certainly never, in a million years, would have expected her to deny her crimes. I cleared my throat and kept my voice even, unsure what to say next.

"If you were innocent of killing Jenny Juliott, why did you confess to the crime?" I asked, tentatively.

"They didn't leave me much choice, did they?" Chrissy snapped, her voice raising defensively.

"Who is 'they'?"

"Them. *You.* The whole god damn town. Not a single

person would have believed it." Chrissy sat back in her seat and sighed.

"Believed what?" my voice a shaky whisper now.

Chrissy leaned forward and I did too. The small gap of desktop between us forgotten.

"That when bad girls lie, good girls die."

I sat back in my chair, exasperated. *What the hell does that mean?*

"Well, if you didn't kill her then who did?"

Chrissy smiled, showing all her teeth for the first time. They were crooked with a distinctive gap, just like the thousands of photos I'd stared at online. There was something ferocious about that smile … something hungry and wild. A chill started at the base of my spine and prickled all the way to my scalp.

Why is she smiling like that?

"The answer is actually pretty obvious if you think about it. I was set up," Chrissy said.

"By whom?" I asked, breathlessly.

I leaned forward again, eager to hear what came next. But the sounds of a blaring car horn outside interrupted us.

"Sorry. I have to go. That's my ride. Dennis."

She stood up and I stood up too.

"You're going already?"

"Yeah. I wanted to meet you first. Size you up. Same time tomorrow?" Chrissy said with a wild grin.

Moments later, I peered through the curtains as a burly

man with a full-sleeve of tattoos led Chrissy through the crowd of reporters, barreling through them and elbowing a path for her.

Size me up. What the hell does that mean?

And who is Dennis?

The tattooed man wrenched open the passenger door of his monster-sized Dodge truck and gave her a boost inside, his hand lingering on the seat of her jeans.

He peeled out of my driveway and moments later, the crowd of reporters were gone. Like the blowflies swarming around Jenny's body, once the corpse was gone, they were too…

Yet one car remained in the gravel drive—a shiny gold Toyota.

Through the window, I stared at the dark-haired woman behind the wheel and she stared back at me. Her eyes were angry green slashes; her rosebud lips puckered up with disdain. *Disdain for me, or for Chrissy? Possibly both…?*

"Go away, Adrianna. Stop posturing," I muttered to myself.

I waited for her to either get out and try to talk to me or leave. I was relieved when she chose the latter.

There was no love lost between us; I couldn't forgive her for turning her back on me. Just like Mom, she gave up on me when I needed an ally.

A smile formed at the corner of my lips as I thought about Adrianna and her dramatic headlines, her ruthless pursuit of her own interests … at least *my* story would be unbiased.

But I don't even know what the whole story is yet … what did Chrissy mean by those words—good girls lie, and bad girls die, or was it the other way around?

Chapter Seven

Through the window of my office, I watched the sun slowly melt beyond the horizon, casting the field in a hellish, firefly radiance that felt less like a warming sunset and more like a warning glow. *This is bad. So bad.*

But why do I feel this bubble of rising excitement? Like today is THE day ... a defining moment that could change the course of my life...?

I wanted to write a book—not just a one-off bestseller, but something that could breathe life into my writing career that had never lifted off the ground...

But not just that: I wanted answers. *What had happened that day in the field? If Chrissy didn't kill Jenny Juliott, then who did? Am I a fool for considering that she might be telling the truth...?*

The glass of whiskey wobbled in my hand as I brought it up to my lips. Knocking it back, I closed my eyes, letting the smoky burn of the Woodford flood my airways and settle hotly in the center of my chest.

But is it worth it? The press and the pressure? The ominous task of getting closer to a potential killer to learn the truth, or at least her version of it? Do I want to know the truth?

Chrissy was gone, our brief first interview concluded hours ago … but part of her still lingered on the other side of my desk: the smell of shampoo and acidic hair dye, the way her personality filled out the entire room when she spoke…

I'd spent the hour jotting down notes. And now, as I gawked at my scratchy writing from earlier, it looked like a nervous splotch of nothingness. Worthless.

In truth, I'd spent most of the hour trying to control my breathing and feigning that I was listening while my heart beat like a wild drum in my chest.

Chrissy showing up at my front door had given me a jolt … *is that why she did it? Perhaps catching the media and me by surprise was exactly what she was going for.*

She'd made a spectacle of it, riling up the press. *Perhaps she'd intended to do that too. But if she's truly innocent, who could blame her?*

I flipped the legal pad over on the desk and poured another glass. I didn't need my notes to remember … it was all etched in my brain, word after shaky word.

And who the hell is this guy she's with, Dennis?

I carried the warm, watery glass of whiskey to my room.

Shivering, I crawled beneath the covers and drained the rest of it.

I can figure out more tomorrow … for now, I need to sleep because Chrissy will be back…

Dennis Alinsky. Mystery solved.

The clock in the lower-right corner of my computer informed me that it was nearly 4am.

Sleep had eluded me for hours. Finally, I'd given in, emerging from bed and finding my way back to my office. No matter how many times I tried to call it my office, it would always be my brother's room.

Jack's bed was gone, and the sturdy oak dressers had been replaced by a heart pine desk and a stiff rosy armchair I'd picked up at Goodwill when I rearranged the room. Nearly ten years he'd been gone…

Head still throbbing from the whiskey earlier, I stared at a picture of Dennis Alinsky online.

Dennis was on Facebook and Twitter too, but he didn't make many posts and his friends list was tiny. A welder by night and motorcycle enthusiast by day (according to his bio), he was originally from Pittsburgh. His family was from there; even his job and motorcycle pals were there.

But Dennis had moved to Austin, Indiana six months ago, renting the empty trailer on Willow Run Road. *The question was: why?*

It took a while to make the connection, but online court documents provided some clarity. The rough and tough biker had no legal problems, but that wasn't the case for his sister Alison.

Alison was his only connection to Indiana, as that was where she was serving her own life sentence. Unlike Chrissy, hers was without parole.

Alison Alinsky, age thirty-four. She had served four years already—her lifelong sentence only just beginning. According to the brief charges listed on the crime database and the more detailed news accounts online, Alison had killed her four-year-old son, Toby.

Alison had held his tiny, unsuspecting head underwater. I pinched my eyes closed and massaged my temples, trying to squeeze the intrusive images of it away.

Alison had denied responsibility. According to her, a shape-shifting demon had entered her home and killed him. A long history of mental health issues and a decent lawyer weren't enough to save her. The jury reached its verdict in little more than an hour.

Because a search of Alison's internet history revealed the truth: that she'd been researching methods of getting rid of her son that ranged from suffocation and poisoning to black market adoption. For his sake, I wish she would have chosen the latter.

Despite the grisly details and eerie appeal of reading up on Alison's case, I couldn't find any connection between her and Chrissy except that they had spent four years in the same maximum-security Indiana prison. *Had they been friends behind bars? Is that how Chrissy came in contact with Alison's brother, Dennis? Did Alison play matchmaker, hooking up her brother with another killer?*

I jotted down a few notes. *I will ask Chrissy about him in the morning and find out what the connection is to Alison.*

I also wanted to know why she was back. *Why not move to Pittsburgh with Dennis if they were dating? Why choose here, the place where all the horror began?*

And her statements to the press claiming her innocence ... *why change the story now? Why not file for an appeal or get another lawyer while still behind bars? Why not fight the charges from the get-go?*

I minimized news articles about the drowning of Toby Alinsky and pulled up the same news video I'd watched a dozen times already.

The angle was different—instead of viewing Chrissy from behind, making her wild statements on my front porch, I saw her from the camera's point of view. Head held high, shoulders thrust back defiantly, she looked straight into the camera and announced our plans of writing her story before we'd ever even discussed it.

A story of innocence, one they'd all have to read if they wanted to know the truth…

It sent chills down my spine, but for some reason I couldn't stop watching. She shimmered in the spotlight, transforming from belligerent social deviant to pitiful, then transforming again to this beautiful, polished, in-control, determined woman who preached from the front steps of the farm where her victim's body had been found.

The strange orange hair actually suited her.

Chrissy's face wasn't the only one in the news. I couldn't bear to watch or read too much … seeing myself on camera, hearing clips of my name and history and connection to the case were overwhelming.

Yes, I wanted the story. But I didn't want the spotlight. And I thought I'd be better prepared.

The media interest wasn't only local either. Sandy Jonas, the host of *Crime Times International*, had reviewed the case on air tonight and mentioned my name. I loved her podcast, but not anymore. I cringed just thinking of her words; they pierced right through me like a knife, twisting my gut pretzel-style and threatening to make me upchuck for the third time tonight.

Sandy, with her sassy know-it-all southern drawl, had said: "At first, I thought: who is this no-name wannabe writer who's been tricked into using her mediocre talents to shine a spotlight on a manipulator like Chrissy Cornwall? But then I made the connection: Breyas. I know that name. Guys, you know it too! Chrissy's victim was discovered on the Breyas farm. And who is this amateur with no writing credits to her name? None other than Natalie Breyas herself. Natalie was only nine years old when Jenny Juliott's body was found on her family's farm. As far as I know, there's been no correspondence between the two women over the years. Yet

Natalie still resides in Austin, Indiana. And get this: she still owns the family farm. As someone who is obsessed with crime, it makes sense to me that this young unemployed woman would be fascinated by Chrissy … by this boogeyman from her youth. She has a degree in creative writing, people! But she's never wrote a book. What the hell does she know about investigative writing? I have some serious concerns. Natalie, honey, if you're listening … don't be fooled by that monster. Chrissy is a sociopath, through and through. She killed that girl and ruined her family's entire life. Hell, in some ways, you could say she ruined yours too. If I remember my history, the brother offed himself many years ago and the mother ran off and skipped town too…"

I turned it off then, my body shaking with … what? Anger, maybe. But mostly humiliation. *I'm not desperate or unemployed. Sandy makes me sound like a desperate loser. And just because I have a degree and no writing credits doesn't mean I can't write well.*

But her words were having more of an effect on me than I would have liked to admit. *Was I foolish to agree to writing this story? I didn't want to help Chrissy if that meant hurting Jenny's family and friends even more than they'd already been hurt…*

Did I make a mistake when I let her in?

What was I thinking when I reached out to her in the first place?

But as much as the public wanted to question my

competence and motives … I still wanted to hear what Chrissy had to say. *Was it morbid curiosity? Maybe.*

But it was something else too … something deeper and darker inside me that wanted to understand how someone who lived only a dozen acres away from me could have turned out so differently.

I wanted to dig deeper, truly understand this "monster", or "boogeyman from my youth" as Sandy Jonas had called her. If she was lying about her innocence, then I'd expose the truth in my book and reveal her as a calculated con-woman in addition to her reputation as a murderer.

And if she's telling the truth … well, the implications of that would be astronomical. Because if Chrissy didn't do it, then someone else did. And reaching for the truth might lead me to another suspect … *and what if I'm wrong, or worse: what if Chrissy's lying and this whole thing has the potential to destroy other people's lives…?*

I stood up from my desk and stretched. My head was still swimming from the whiskey earlier; my eyes heavy with sleep and my lower back achy from leaning over during my talk with Chrissy and while scrolling online endlessly for hours.

The sun would be up in a few hours and Chrissy would return. I needed to be ready this time—*this is my chance to prove myself and to get to the bottom of the truth.*

Chapter Eight

But nine o'clock came and went, and Chrissy never showed. It was impossible to hide my disappointment and restlessness as I glanced through the blinds for the hundredth time, still hoping she might turn up.

I'd expected the media to come again too. But neither Chrissy nor any reporters showed up this morning. *Where is everyone?*

Finally, as eleven o'clock approached, I took a shower and choked down a tunafish sandwich before heading in for my shift at Kmart. If Chrissy turned up late while I was at work, so be it. *She should have been on time.*

It was a dreary Saturday, the last of the month. Not a sliver of sun in the sky. Bulgy black storm clouds hovered, following me on my twenty-minute drive to work.

Reminding me of the demons Alison Alinsky claimed were following her and her son...

I tried to focus on the monotonous curvy roadways, passing churches and graveyards—it's all brimstone and death in this town—until I emerged in the center of Austin. But my mind was still on Chrissy. *Why didn't she show like she promised this morning? Did she change her mind?* After all of the negative news coverage following her speech yesterday, my own decision had certainly wavered. *What if another writer approached her, promising money or offering a more supportive ear?*

But I remembered her words from yesterday: *who better than me to tell it?*

Fat pellets of rain showered down on the car as I parked in my usual spot. Kmart was connected to several other small facilities—Dollar Tree, a rent-by-the-month furniture store, and the food stamp office. For a Saturday, the parking lot was mostly deserted, only a few cars parked out front. One of them, a smart red Firebird, belonged to my boss Shane.

I waited a few minutes, hoping the rain might die down. I didn't own an umbrella, or a rain jacket for that matter. But when I saw no signs of slowing, I thrust the driver's side door open and ran across the parking lot, Reeboks squeaking on the grimy pavement.

When it came to my personality and skills, there were many things lacking. But one thing I did have going for me: I was punctual and I liked to think that my loyalty and responsibility helped make up for my lack of people skills.

Shane had never called me his favorite, but it was obvious that I was. He always encouraged my fellow co-workers to imitate my work ethic and this fact didn't score me any friend points at work.

I shook my long brown hair, goosebumps sprouting as my damp skin came in contact with the air conditioning that always seemed to be running in this place.

Maryann and Sharon were working the two registers in the front. I waved at them and smiled, still shaking water from my hair as I walked to the back of the store to punch my time-card.

Ten years ago, when the farm became mine, I thought this job would be temporary. By now, I should be married with 2.5 kids and a decent job that required a degree … but the mess with Jack had left me frozen in time, a temporary suspension in Austin.

This might be all there ever is, I thought, looking around at the depressing fluorescent lights and the store's Halloween display.

"Natalie, there you are," Regina said in her sing-songy voice as I scanned my employee badge and waited for the ding to confirm I was punched in correctly and on time.

I turned around and feigned a smile. "Here I am," I replied, dully. Regina was kind, but nosey, and she usually only worked a few days a week. I'd heard a rumor that she wanted to go full-time but couldn't because of my position.

She has two kids and really needs the money, Maryann had told me. As though, just because I hadn't given birth, I didn't need money to eat and pay bills.

Regina was sweeping up the break area, guiding a hill of crumbs and dust into her thick gray dust bin.

"Shane wants to see you. I told him I'd send you in." She busied herself with the broom and her tiny tower of crumbs.

"Oh really? Okay, thanks." I wedged my purse inside my employee locker and made my way down the long black hall that led to the storage bay and my boss's office.

His door was open as usual.

I watched him for a few seconds, head bent low over a stack of invoices, and admired his chiseled jaw and his stylish red hair. I knocked on the door frame.

"Good morning."

"Morning. Come in." He waved me in with barely a glance up from his papers.

Shane was younger than any other boss I'd had—barely over thirty. He was handsome. His unruly hair was strangely attractive; his eyes green with little specks of gold in them. He always wore nice fitted shirts, but sometimes, I could see a sliver of a dragon tattoo peeking out from his right bicep.

He was too young for me, not to mention my boss ... but I'd fantasized about him a few times since starting here. He was kind and handsome, with those underlying bad boy tones.

I caught myself licking my lips as I stared at his. *How long has it been since I've been with a man?* I tried to rewind the clock and count back ... *a year, maybe? Probably closer to two.*

I'd gone on a couple dates since moving to Austin, but nothing beyond dinner and sex. And in college, most of the neighbors in my apartment complex were either married or old.

I'll never meet a man in this town, I thought, drearily. *But maybe ... if I'm busy with my new writing career, I won't mind it.*

I frowned when I saw Shane's expression. He looked ... *concerned.* Angry, possibly. *What the hell?* I'd seen him irritated with some of my co-workers, but never me.

And that's when it hit me: the news coverage. My name and face splashed all over the local news, not to mention my "mention" on a popular international podcast. *What might he think of me after seeing and hearing all that?*

Fear bloomed in my chest as I considered something worse than losing his acceptance: *is he going to fire me because of all this?*

His eyebrows furrowed, then he asked, "Are you doing okay, Natalie?"

As fond of me as Shane seemed and despite my minor crush on him, he rarely asked me direct, personal questions.

"Yeah. Doing great. Thanks for asking," I said, awkwardly.

"Because I heard about what happened … and I'm a little concerned. Are you holding up okay?"

I released a breath, the comforting concern in his voice easing my nerves slightly.

"I'm okay. A little overwhelmed by all this, but fine."

I sat down across from him, letting out an anxious whoosh of breath as I settled in the chair.

Shane nodded slowly, taking this in. I wasn't sure if he believed me.

"Are you really going to write that woman's story? I mean, I knew you liked to write, but I had no idea that true crime was something that interested you. It's a little macabre, don't you think?"

I'm doing it because … well, I guess it's because I'm in that second group of people, the kind that slow down and look at tragedy. It's not because I enjoy the macabre; it's because I'm SO affected by it. I can't look away—there's no choice in the matter. I have to know the truth, down to the gritty details.

"Don't you think, Natalie?" Shane repeated, shaking me out of my trance.

"Well, I'm not planning on leaving Kmart if that's what you mean. But we did set up an interview to discuss it. I promise that I won't let it interfere with my job," I said, wistfully. By "we", I meant Chrissy and me, but I didn't dare say her name. This town hated her name.

Shane smiled and again, I felt a small flicker of relief.

"You're a great employee, Natalie. One my best. Actually, you probably are *the* best."

My cheeks warmed. "Thank you, sir. That means a lot."

His grin evaporated.

"That's why this is so hard..."

Oh no.

And that's when I knew it: *I'm losing my job! All because of this stupid media coverage...*

"Please don't do this. I really need the money," I whined. It was true: I did. Even though the pay wasn't great, it was steady. And I needed a regular income to pay my bills and keep the farm.

"Natalie," he said, steepling his fingers pensively. I'd never heard him say my name so many times in one day. Frankly, I didn't like it.

"I didn't bring you in here to fire you. I don't care what anyone says—you're an exemplary employee. But I've received word from the higher-ups ... Annie from Corporate has asked me to give you a couple weeks off until the circus dies down. There have been complaints and they are concerned about their reputation."

Annie from Corporate. I don't even know who that is.

"What sort of complaints?" I asked, nervously.

"From a couple employees and customers ... they're threatening to quit or boycott the store if we don't let you go."

"I thought you said..."

"I'm *not* firing you. All I'm asking for is a couple weeks ... cooperate with me here. It's just until things blow over.

The last thing we need is some sort of circus around here, making us look bad."

"But…"

"And you know the store is already struggling. I can't afford for *all of us* to lose our jobs over this, Natalie."

"Paid or unpaid?" The question was pointless. I already knew the answer.

"Unpaid." Shane grimaced.

"Fine. It doesn't sound like I have much of a choice here." I stood up, eyes glistening with tears. I swiped at my face, hating myself for coming across as weak in front of him.

"Seriously, you know how much I like you. You're a great employee…"

"Thanks, Shane. I've got to go." I scurried out of his office, the need to let loose all my hot wet tears leaving me breathless. There was a knot in my throat, thickening by the second. *I have to get out of here. NOW.*

Regina was still in the break room, sweeping up an invisible pile of dirt. She was humming, a tiny smile forming at the corners of her lips.

I'm sure Regina will be more than willing to cover my shifts for me.

I held my head down as I grabbed my things from my locker and went back outside, a gush of wind and crispy dead leaves pinwheeling around me as I crossed the parking lot.

The media wasn't outside, and I probably won't even

see Chrissy again! *And now I have to spend two weeks, unpaid, off work because of this bogus bullshit. And why didn't she show up this morning?! I need this fucking job...*

———————

Twenty minutes later, I was back at the farm. I threw my purse and windbreaker on the sofa then charged up the stairs to my office.

What am I going to do all week, now that I'm off work and Chrissy changed her mind? Maybe if I make a public statement—that I'm not *writing the book—they'll let me come back to work and earn my paycheck...*

My computer screen was lit up, my email open. I narrowed my eyes at it. *What the hell? I thought I shut the computer down this morning before I left.*

I was usually so good about logging out and shutting it down, doing it most evenings as though on auto-pilot.

I glanced around my office, a strange wisp of paranoia settling in. *Did someone break in, go through my emails...?*

But as my eyes scanned the room, I couldn't see anything out of place. No one had rummaged through my desk or closet ... nothing was out of the ordinary, besides the lit-up computer screen.

I did a quick walk through the rest of the second-floor rooms, feeling strangely foolish.

I must have left it on or accidentally hit restart. It wouldn't be the first time I've done that. Plus, I was pretty distracted and hung over this morning.

I took a seat in the soft leather desk chair, my eyes scanning through emails, only briefly registering advertisements and social media notifications. I stopped on an unopened email that looked like it had come from a personal account: scapegoat227 at yahoo.

The subject line had been left blank.

Scapegoat. Is that what she thinks she is? But … a scapegoat for who?

I clicked on the email, noting that it had arrived at 7:30 this morning.

Hi Natalie,

I don't know much about email but here is mine. Can't meet you this morning. There are a dozen reporters camped outside and most have been here all night. Can we meet tonight instead? I was thinking you could come here. Are you cool with that? Dennis works 3rd shift so we can get some quiet time to do the interview. Can you come around 11pm?

C

Eleven o'clock at night? I mean, it's not like I had to work tonight, but I wasn't sure how I felt about meeting on Chrissy's own turf … and that late at night. Would it be safe there?

There was no point in mulling it over—my mind was already made up. I wrote her back, keeping my message brief:

See you at 11.

Compared to the sanctuary of my family farm, Dennis's trailer looked downright desolate. It was silent and dark; a rusty old double-wide with a broken-down Chrysler parked haphazardly in the grass out front. It was a secluded lot, set back from the road and surrounded by trees on all sides. I looked around for a motorcycle but didn't see one.

The gravel driveway was empty of cars; no media around, much to my relief.

I wonder how she got the media to leave. Maybe, hopefully, they gave up for the night ... thinking Dennis was gone and that Chrissy had gone to bed.

I pulled into the gravel drive, my heart in my throat as the tires spun, kicking up gravel and dust. I took a deep breath and forced myself to get out of the car. *Was coming here a mistake?*

I kept my eyes on the trailer as I went around to the passenger side of my car and scooped up my heavy bag of notes, tape recorder, and the letter opener (just in case), which I tucked in my back jeans pocket.

I swung the bag over my right shoulder and followed a

rickety wheelchair ramp up to the front door. As I approached, I could see two soft lights glowing from inside.

I raised my hand to knock just as the door swung open.

Chrissy stood in the dimly lit doorway; hair piled messily in a bun on top of her head. She looked … *sleepy*.

"Should I come back or…?" My throat was dry, tongue like sandpaper sticking to the roof of my mouth. I chastised myself for not bringing along a bottle of water or breath mints.

"No, of course not. Get in here," Chrissy barked. She shoved the screen wider, looking past me toward the empty driveway and road beyond.

As soon as I was inside, she closed and bolted the door behind me.

"Fooled them, didn't we?" she said with a chuckle.

"Who? The media?"

"Who else? Those pestering assholes didn't expect you to come here. And the house has been pitch dark for hours. They finally pulled out about an hour ago. I was worried I'd have to cancel on you again. Come on…" As I followed Chrissy through a dark living room and through an archway into a cramped eat-in kitchen, I couldn't help noticing how nice the interior of the trailer was. Sure, it was old and sparse, but it looked clean and well taken care of. The sink and counters were sparkling, the couch and armchair in the living room worn but cared-for.

Chrissy settled into a seat at the table, nodding for me to take a seat too.

"I brought a tape recorder. Is that okay? It's to help me review later ... while I'm writing." I don't know why I expected her to refuse, but she simply shrugged and shook out a pack of Camels from her loose-fitting sweatpants. She lit a cigarette then offered me the pack.

"No, thank you," I said, tempted to take one anyway. It had been nearly four years since I'd smoked one and the peppery cloud of smoke that filled my lungs burned with intensity, and memories of times long gone...

"Just a sec." Chrissy stood and shuffled to the counter, flipping off all the kitchen lights except a yellowish heat lamp by the stove. "That's better," she sighed, slipping back in her chair. She took a long drag from her cigarette and blew a ring of smoke in my direction. I didn't flinch; instead, I stared down the convicted murderer, determined to get the truth once and for all. *She doesn't scare me. I won't let her manipulate me. There's more to this story—I know there is.*

In the dimly lit room, Chrissy's features had softened, taking on a youthful, heady glow. The crinkles around her mouth, the scar on her cheek, were barely visible in the dark. Briefly, I could almost believe she was the girl again—the young thuggish girl in her mugshot photo—not the old, sad woman they hauled out of prison...

I stared down at my tape recorder. It felt too stiff, unnatural. For now, I decided not to use it.

"Were you born in Austin? There's so much about your teenage years online ... but nothing much about before."

Chrissy smiled. "Sure was. What a shitty place to grow up in, am I right?"

She erupted with laughter that quickly morphed into coughing.

"What about your family? Can you tell me a bit about them?"

Chrissy frowned, eyes growing distant as she thought about her life before.

"Well, I had two brothers. Both older than me. Trevor and Trent."

"Did you get along?" I pressed.

Chrissy shrugged, stubbed out her cigarette, then immediately reached for another.

"Like I said, they were older. Trevor was four years older and Trent was six. They were closer with each other than they were with me. Dad was a truck driver. Gone most of the time." She narrowed her eyes wistfully through the smoke.

"And your mother?" I'd seen photos of Ruby Juliott—she'd looked like an older, skinnier version of Chrissy now.

"She stayed home with us and she loved the boys. They were her everything."

I searched Chrissy's face for traces of bitterness or jealousy but found none.

"Didn't she love you too?"

Chrissy stubbed out her half-smoked cigarette and pushed the chair back, startling me.

"Well, of course she did. She was my mother after all."

She walked over to the refrigerator, opened it up with a bang and peered inside it. "What would you like to drink? Soda, milk … beer?"

My stomach still raw from last night's whiskey, I surprised myself by saying, "I'll have a beer, please." *Anything to take the edge off.*

Chrissy took out a Miller Lite and popped the top, then walked over and sat it down in front of me. She poured herself a glass of milk, hands shaky as she did so. I wanted to ask more questions—mainly, why she'd confessed to the murder she now claimed she didn't commit.

"Look." Chrissy took a long swig of milk, coating her upper lip. She belched loudly, then got up and poured the rest down the sink. "Can we skip some of the early questions?"

For someone who had just spent half her life in prison, I felt a little insulted by the fact that she was "bored". But I had to admit, my stiff line of questioning wasn't going anywhere.

"I know it's hard to talk about family. It's hard for me too. But these details are important … readers will want to know all about your background when they read the book. It's important to get the full picture," I explained.

Chrissy waved a hand at me and came back over to the table to sit down. "Fine. Ask me more. But then can I just talk for a while?"

"Sure," I conceded.

I cleared my throat. Already, she had thrown me off my

CARISSA ANN LYNCH

game. If asking my initial questions had made me nervous earlier, now I was downright uncomfortable.

"Your mother homeschooled you and your siblings. What was that like for you?"

Chrissy chuckled. "I know what you heard. That the Cornwall kids were nothing but trash and our parents couldn't afford to send us to school."

I shook my head. "That's not what I heard. Remember, I was young when all of this went down, Chrissy. I don't know…"

But she was exactly right—that is what I'd heard.

"But you heard plenty else probably. Did they tell you that my father beat us? That my mama was a prostitute on drugs? That CPS came out a few times, but never had cause to take us?"

Rattled, I put down my pen and gave her my full attention.

"There are many stories, Chrissy. But I want to know your version. The real version … because that's the only one that matters right now. I don't know if you did it or not, but this case has always haunted me. And frankly, I never bought the idea that you killed her all by yourself. You were just a child."

Chrissy's face softened, her limbs loosening as she leaned back in her chair.

"My daddy never beat us. And I never saw my mom with no other men…"

I waited for her to say more.

"But the drugs ... that part was sort of true. Mom's brother, my uncle Joey, he was a dealer then. Mom offered to help him; I guess we needed the money. But then something went wrong, as it does when you deal with that shit. She got herself hooked on pain pills."

"How did Joey react?" His name ping-ponged around my brain ... I wasn't familiar with him. Had any of the other books or online articles made mention of Chrissy's uncle...?

"He was pissed. See, they weren't real brother and sister. Mom's mom died when she was young, and Joey's mom raised her as her own daughter. So, I think there was already some resentment there."

"What did he do when he realized she was dipping into the stash they were supposed to be selling?" I pressed.

"He showed up drunk one night. Dad wasn't home; he never was. Joey beat the hell out of Mom. Gave the boys a good ass-kicking too."

"And you? What did he do to you?"

Chrissy's smile was shaky. She took a long, slow drag of her cigarette, then said, "What do you think he did?"

I could only imagine the number of creepy things shitty mean uncles might do to a young, vulnerable girl like Chrissy...

"I'm so sorry that happened to you."

Chrissy's solemn expression spread into a wide smile, then she shocked me with a snort of laughter.

"I'm messing with you, Nat. He didn't lay a hand on me.

My uncle was many things, but he wasn't a pervert. And although he beat the boys and Mom too, I was never a part of that. I was his favorite and when he left me that night, cleaning up blood and knocked-over furniture from the fight, he told me: 'Chrissy, try to get them in line, would ya?'"

Chrissy cackled, and coughed, eyes fuzzy as she thought back to that day.

Her laughter was strange, and so out of place, but I couldn't help seeing it for what it was: a way to deflect the pain. Chrissy grew up rough and I'd always known that, but hearing it from her felt different. I could see the pain she was trying to hide behind the tough exterior and the inappropriate laughing.

For the first time since meeting the real Chrissy Cornwall in person, I tried to imagine her doing all those things they said. Memories of Jenny's bloated face from the crime photos ... the knife wounds on her neck and back ... the burn marks on her hands and face...

My stomach curled in on itself as I considered that she might be just as guilty as everyone said.

But still, I don't quite believe that.

Chrissy reached for her pack of smokes again, studying my face as it became clear.

"Look, I know it's strange that I can laugh about it now. But when you grow up the way we did, you have to find humor in the stupid shit. Weeks later, my daddy broke Joey's nose in a bar brawl, and then the next thing we knew, he was coming around to apologize to mama, and to the boys. They all mended their ways and Joey got out of the drug business. Years later they would laugh about that night … I guess that's why I'm laughing too."

I thought about what it might be like—really like—growing up as a Cornwall in Austin. Sure, my family was poor. But Chrissy's family took it to another level, and they never apologized for it.

"Tell me about John Bishop."

Chrissy took a drag and narrowed her eyes, thinking for a minute before she spoke.

"The papers said I was obsessed with him, but it was him who pursued me…"

"Were you boyfriend and girlfriend?" It sounded so childish saying it that way, but I didn't know how else to ask. According to the media, John had been dating both girls.

"Boys like John Bishop didn't date girls like me. They dated girls like Jenny Juliott. The only thing he wanted from me was sex," Chrissy said, bitterly.

Thinking back to pictures of John and Jenny as a couple … even in the dead of winter, John had this dog days of summer tan—golden brown and healthy, his hair white hot like it was bleached by rays of the sun. And Jenny … she was even more noticeable. With her hitched-up skirts, narrow waist, and voluptuous curves she reminded us all of a playboy bunny. Her skin was tan, her beachy waves golden blonde to match John's. But despite her grotesque beauty, she was lovely and kind, and just as smart as she was sweet. She was what the papers and stories would call "the girl next door".

But I guess that all depends on who lives next door. For me, through the field and across the creek was a wild and rambunctious girl who was pretty but dirty, attractive but damaged ... Chrissy was "the girl next door" to my family.

When the news broke of Jenny's death, I saw so many ludicrous headlines. They didn't really bother me until I was older, until I was wise enough to get it, to finally understand how the world worked...

"Too pretty to die" read one of the headlines. *As though ugly people are more deserving of murder...*

And another: "What could have been—Jenny Juliott's Potential". It was an article in *Fifteen* magazine ... an analysis by a "modeling expert" that went on to claim Jenny had had everything they were looking for. Perfect skin and cheekbones ... the height, weight, and unique presence needed to make it onto the runway.

As though somehow her potential in modeling made her death more meaningful ... Jenny was smart, but nobody ever mentioned that in their articles. It was all about her skin and her cheekbones ... her shocking baby blue eyes...

"What are you thinking about?"

I jumped at the sound of Chrissy's voice; her question sounded so intimate and she was leaning across the table, her hand stretching toward mine, so close I could almost feel her odd vibrations bursting from her fingertips and seeping into my own…

"I was remembering Jenny," I said, earnestly.

"Ah. Yes, Jenny…"

"You knew they were dating. I mean, yes … you were homeschooled. But everyone in Austin knew that John and Jenny were a couple. Can you tell me how you and John met? When did it start between you…?"

Chrissy said, "Well, I'm sure you know what they said in the papers. What the prosecutors said in court…"

I nodded. I did. But I wanted to hear it from her.

"It was summer when I went to the party with Trevor. My brother was older, like I said, so he hung out with a lot of kids much older than me. See, unlike me and Trent … Trevor was bitter because he wanted to go to school. He liked hanging out with those silly rich kids, no offense."

I certainly wouldn't call most of them "rich kids". My brother and I didn't fit that bill at all. But, in Chrissy's eyes, I could see how she saw it that way…

"Truth be told, they couldn't stand Trevor. But you know why they liked him around?"

I took a long sip of my lukewarm beer. When I realized she was waiting for me to ask, I swallowed and said, "No. Why?"

"Trevor could fight. And if there were one thing those snotty-ass kids liked to do when they got drunk it was having a good brawl in the front yard. Beating Trevor was the gold standard, you see. Not a single one of them could do it."

"What did your brother get out of it?"

Chrissy snorted. "That fucker loved to fight. Still does probably…"

"Do you still communicate with your family?"

Chrissy's teasing smile evaporated. "No."

"They didn't come to see you in prison?"

She shook her head.

"Not even once?"

Chrissy put up a finger. "Once. My father came. I could see it in his eyes when he sat down … the horror and the shame he felt, seeing his baby girl behind bars."

"What did he say?"

"It was me who did all the talking. I told him and Mom to move on, my brothers too … to let me do my time in peace. Jenny's time with her family was over; didn't seem fair for me to get to see mine."

"That doesn't sound like something an innocent person would say, no offense." The words flowed like honey from my tongue, the beer loosening me up already. "I'm sorry," I added, scooting the drink away with my fingertips.

Chrissy frowned. "No, you're right. It doesn't. It's exactly what a guilty person would say. But I never denied feeling bad about what happened to Jenny. Guilt and remorse … do you really think the person who did all those terrible things to her was capable of feeling regret?"

Flashes of crime scene photos bombarded my memories

... and the real view—the only one that mattered ... her wounds jagged and deep, the burn marks on her face and hands. *No, whoever did that is pure evil,* I decided.

Chrissy seemed gloomy and headstrong, a woman with a dark past.

But a killer? I just can't see it.

"We got off-track for a second. We were talking about how you met John," I recalled.

Chrissy smiled. "Ah yes. John Bishop. How could I forget? I met him at a party with Trevor. He didn't like to take me with him, but sometimes he had to ... when my mom tried to get her shit together, she took a night job. It was great 'cause it meant we had a steady income and she was staying clean ... but Dad was still out on the road a lot, so my brothers had to take care of me. Trent was older, with his own friends by then, which meant I was left in the care of Trevor most nights."

"Did your mom know you were going to those parties?"

Chrissy shrugged. "I don't think so, but what choice did she have? My brother wouldn't have listened to her even if she had forbade him to take me."

"And John?" I pressed.

"John ... he was a pretty boy; I'll give him that. But he was way too stuck up for me."

"But you all did date..." I pressed.

"All you school brats ... you had to put a name to everything. The truth is that I wasn't into him at first. It was all him, constantly asking me to come hang out. Writing notes. I wanted no part of it, honestly. But, then, finally ... I agreed to hang out with him one-on-one."

This didn't ring true to me either. In every story and article I'd read, Chrissy was supposedly obsessed with John and hated his steady girlfriend, Jenny...

"What made you change your mind and agree to see him?" I asked, going along with her version of the story.

"He grew on me, I guess. But that was before I got to see the real side of him. He rarely saw Jenny outside of school; did you know that?"

I did. Jenny Juliott was a preacher's daughter. The way she was raised was probably the complete opposite of Chrissy Cornwall.

"I think I did know that," I said, quietly.

The real side of John Bishop. What did that entail? The papers had made him out to be the popular kid ... the all-American athlete with good grades and a killer smile. The kind of boy girls would kill for...

"I don't think John had ever met a girl like me. I smoked and drank. I wasn't afraid to mess around ... and I wasn't stuck up like Jenny. After she found out he liked me, she started smoking and even trying to dress like me ... you probably don't believe me."

"No, I do. I'm just taking it all in. According to the news it was you who pursued him..."

"They lied. But does it matter? The results were the same. A girl still wound up dead," Chrissy said, solemnly.

Her eyes were glassy, a gleam to them I hadn't seen before.

"It might matter. If someone set you up, Chrissy ... or you know who really did this ... you should tell me," I spoke, softly.

Chrissy yawned. "I'm tired. Is it okay if we talk more tomorrow? I'll shoot you an email when I'm free."

I'd be lying if I said I wasn't disappointed. It was midnight, but I could have listened to Chrissy talk all night...

"No problem. Just let me know." I picked up the unused tape recorder and closed my notebook.

"I have something for you to look at when you get home. Wait here," Chrissy said.

She stood and sauntered down a dark hallway. For a brief moment, I imagined her emerging from the shadows ... a dark silhouette wielding a big bloody knife in her hands...

It was hard to separate the Chrissy now from the Chrissy in the stories. She didn't seem dangerous to me, but how could I know for sure?

When she returned, Chrissy was carrying a crusty old shoebox. "Don't lose any of this, okay? I've been saving this stuff forever."

I took the box from her hands. I was tempted to lift the lid but didn't.

"Okay. Talk to you tomorrow," I said.

I saw myself out, watching from my seat in the driveway as all the lights in the trailer dimmed, one by one. The box was on the passenger seat, calling my name. Perhaps there would be some good bits and pieces I could use in my interview, or even pics I could include inside the book.

As I drove home, listening to sad songs on the radio, I was smiling despite myself. My thoughts were swirling with visions of my future book. *Could I do it? Turn out a real, readable story about the murder of Jenny Juliott?* I imagined what it would look like—bold, catchy title on the front and glossy, never-before-seen photos on the inside…

As much as I wanted to indulge in my fantasy of seeing a book with my name on it, what I wanted more than anything right now was answers. More than answers … I wanted the truth.

Chapter Nine

The wind was vicious as I climbed out of my car, gripping my keys in one hand and balancing the old shoe box in the other. From the gravel drive, the farmhouse looked sad and abandoned. I'd forgotten to flip the porch light on when I'd left in a hurry; it looked silent and dark, an empty house in an empty field under a sad, empty night sky.

The only light to guide my path to the front door was the cold white moon hovering above the field.

Once upon a time, the field had been teeming with crops and farm equipment. The bright red pole barn, where my dad used to spend so much of his free time, was lopsided and streaked with mold. My brother had lain new gravel inside it, but it was rickety and swaying ... the whole thing needed new paint, new walls ... or maybe it just needed to be torn down completely. It wasn't like I used it anymore.

The field stretched on and on, the grass overgrown but dried out, the split-level fence swaying dangerously in the wind. The farm was a forgotten wasteland. In the distance, trees formed a line between our property and that of the Cornwalls. Only the Cornwalls had been gone for many years now, the old trailer empty and ghostlike, hidden beyond the trees.

The trees, too, swayed dangerously in the breeze, their branches reaching like gnarly old hands … reaching for me, accusing me. *How could you help this woman?*

I stumbled up to the front porch, teeth chattering from the cold, and after a few tries, I was able to slip my key in correctly and let myself inside.

I flipped on switches in the living room and kitchen, setting the place aglow, chasing away faceless ghosts…

I dropped the shoe box on the kitchen table, giving it one last leery look before trotting to my bedroom to fetch my robe. The inside of the farmhouse wasn't much warmer than the cold elements outside. I checked the thermostat. Barely sixty.

Damn heater's going out again.

In my bedroom, I slipped on my ratty black robe that used to be Dad's. It was motheaten and frayed, but it was thick, warm, and comforting. *I need that now.*

I twisted my hair in a tight knot on top of my head and returned to the box in the kitchen. I had an idea of what might be inside—photos, probably—or perhaps court documents that Chrissy had saved.

The clock on the stove revealed it was almost one in the morning, but I couldn't sleep without taking a look. I took a seat and peeled back the lid, instantly hit by the smell of something dusty and sweet, like old fruit.

The first thing I saw was an envelope, unlabeled. After peeking under the fold, I realized I was right about one thing—these were definitely pictures. Nearly a dozen old polaroids were tucked inside the envelope. Gently, I removed the stack then spread the photos out like a fan across my kitchen table.

The first photo was of a girl, barely five or six. I recognized her immediately. Lips as pale as her skin, she was wearing a tired smile, the gap between her front teeth already prominent.

The photo of Chrissy was old, the details of her face pixelated and dull. But there was an eerie stillness to it; and I thought to myself: this photo would look great in the mid-section of my book when it's done.

But there was something else too—the innocence of her smile, the wide-eyed excitement in her eyes. Chrissy had been a little girl just like me, poor but full of promise. *How did it all go wrong?*

That was the only picture of Chrissy by herself … the rest were of various family members—Trevor and Trent, I presumed—a young dark-haired toddler and another boy with dark hair who was only six or seven. And then there were two of the entire family—Ruby and Alec Cornwall, with a boy on either side of them, and a plump-faced infant in an old-fashioned dress and bonnet ensemble on Ruby's lap. I stared at the bright eyes and playful smile ... it's hard to imagine that someone so innocent, so sweet, could commit such a heinous act. It might have been cut and dried for the rest of Austin, but I always felt like there was so much more... Maybe it's because I was so young and didn't get all the details, but it felt like there was something missing.

Chrissy was so young and innocent; the perfect scapegoat for the crime.

But, as I knew from reading true life crime stories, sometimes the most obvious explanation was the *right* one. Chrissy did seem to be the only one back then with a motive.

And don't forget the confession, I reminded myself, warily.

I flipped through a few more photos, unable to shake off the feeling that they could be my very own ... a young happy family doing what young happy families do ... birthday parties and Easter. The kids at Christmas, huddled around the tree on their knees, grinning at boxes with bows, while the adults smiled jovially on the couch.

Carefully, I stacked the delicate old photos and slid them back inside their envelope and took a deep breath. It was strange seeing Chrissy in her family element; there had been hundreds of photos of her over the years in the paper and on the internet, but they had been mostly photos of her as a teen and adult. Seeing her real life felt like something different ... she looked so young and normal.

And her family photos brought back an aching want for my own. Mine weren't lost, merely stored away—there were two plastic tubs filled with my own family's albums and loose photos in the cellar of the farmhouse. I had looked at them only once since moving back home—but I didn't look for long, and I hadn't looked since.

Did we look as happy as the Cornwalls did in their photos? And most importantly: could you tell a difference between before and after ... before the dead girl showed up in our field, and after we found her?

Dad had grown distant and quieter. Jack immersed himself in his own little world in his room. And Mom... When I closed my eyes, I could still see her, locket swinging around her neck as she chased me through the rows of corn. Hair silver like the moon.

We were happy once. All of us. But then everything fell apart...

Dad buried his feelings and Mom ran away with hers ... and Jack ... well, Jack stayed busy, but perhaps ... perhaps it all caught up with him in the end. How much of his suicide is related to the past? *Perhaps, like me, he never fully recovered from the tragedy and Mom leaving...*

When I opened my eyes, refocusing on Chrissy's box, a cold chill ran up my spine. I tucked my hands in my long robe sleeves, using them as gloves to handle the rest of the contents of the box.

Something more interesting was tucked beneath the photos ... three handwritten notes, each meticulously folded in that playful, old-school way that made my heart throb with nostalgia. I used to be able to do it, but for the life of me I couldn't remember how.

Slowly, I untucked the corners and carefully unraveled the first one. The letter was written on notebook paper, the scratchy print letters immediately reminding me of a guy's handwriting, not a girl's.

My Dear Sweet Chrissy,

I can still taste that minty Chapstick you were wearing on your lips last Saturday. I miss you. I told you to call me. Why haven't you? I know you said I'm not you're type, but guess what? You're not my type either. Maybe that's why we are perfect together. Like that couple, Romeo and Juliet. Please come this weekend. I want to be alone with you.

Love always,

John

The second note was folded more tightly. The paper felt dusty and thin between my fingers, as though it might fall away at any moment, evaporating into dust. Taking its precious words with it...

This one was written in sloppy cursive.

CHRISSY,

Come on. Sneak out and meet me tonight. Let's have our own party, beautiful. —J

Carefully, I plucked up the last letter and untucked the folded edges. The handwriting in this one was neater ... and strangely, more feminine.

Blinking sleep from my eyes, I read through the lines several times then placed all three letters neatly back in the box. There was more inside ... an Austin Elementary School yearbook, some more loose photos...

I'll look at it all more thoroughly tomorrow, I decided. My eyes were heavy with sleep and I closed the lid on the box and carried it back to my room. Giving it one last rueful glance, I placed it beside my bed on the nightstand.

My bed still unmade from this morning, I nudged the covers aside and lay down on top of the sheets. The house was still chilly, the robe strangely constricting ... yet I was too tired to take it off.

Eyes closed, my mind swirled with thoughts ... mostly, they were stuck on the contents of that third letter. Something about those words had chilled me to the bone. *Was Jenny the one who sent it?*

Chrissy—

I heard about what happened and please let me say: I'm not angry with you. It's not your fault and I don't blame you. The person at fault is John. Thank you for telling me the truth and being honest. I'm going to confront him about it tomorrow.

JJ

Chapter Ten

When I opened my eyes, my body was shaking. At first, I presumed it was from the cold ... the heater still barely putting off any heat. But then I realized ... I was sweating. Remnants of a dream slivered through my mind, snaking their way back out ... too fast. Always too fast to hold onto...

I glanced over at the closed blinds, surprised to find darkness seeping through the cracks. Although I liked to get up early, I rarely rose before the sun.

Blinking, I rolled over onto my side and reached for my phone. I usually kept it on the nightstand, but now there was only the crumbling shoe box that Chrissy had given me last night.

I groaned. Untwisted myself from the sheets.

As I stumbled through the hallway and toward the kitchen, in search of my cell phone, it dawned on me that it wasn't morning. When I reached the kitchen, the angry red numbers on the stove told me it wasn't even 4am.

Great. I slept for less than three hours. What the hell?

Reaching the table, I pressed the home button on my iPhone. I stared at the home screen—a generic beach scene with sand and white caps—it was indeed only 4am. *So what woke me?*

A deep sleeper, I rarely rose without an alarm. But, lately, my body had been on edge—always ready to leap up and bounce at every single shadow and sound.

Acting on a hunch, I moved to the living room window and peeked through the blinds. I don't know what I was expecting—*the press on my doorstep at four in the morning? Chrissy Cornwall on the front porch?*

But there was nothing in the driveway besides my car, parked crooked from when I'd driven home from Chrissy's only a few hours earlier.

But something about it wasn't right. A yellowish reflection of the moon on my windshield … *no, that's not it. Something's out there … something's not right*, I realized.

I unlatched the bolt and, nervously, pushed the front door open a crack. I listened for the sounds of the countryside—coyotes rummaging through the field, raccoons tearing through the garbage cans … but heard nothing.

Then there it was … the tinkling sound of a bell, or a wind chime. Maybe even a young child's laughter…

I pushed the door open and stepped out onto the porch.

I was in my robe and I wasn't wearing shoes, but I had to see for myself. Had to chase away the boogeyman …

"Hello?" I called out cautiously, looking left toward the country road and then right toward the field.

I couldn't see the moon anymore, the night sky star-free and full of sickle-shaped angry clouds. *Where did the yellow light I saw come from?* I wondered.

But that's when I heard it: the unmistakable sound of laughter, but it was so far away … carried from afar on the wind. I cupped my hands around my mouth. "Who's out there? This is private property," I bellowed.

I could have sworn I heard the sharp sound of a gasp in the distance and then the yellow flash of a handheld light poking through the trees …

There was someone running through the field, the quiet thump of their shoes … and then the rustling of trees in the distance. *What the hell?*

"Who's out there?" I bellowed.

Impulsively, I stepped off the porch, my bare feet instantly met with the sharp, unforgiving gravel. I winced, but took a few more steps anyway and flipped on my flashlight app.

Holding it out in front of me like a spotlight, I moved it left to right, shining it all along the tree line, looking for trespassers. When I didn't see anyone, I swept my light over the field…

I stopped when my light hit a lumpy shadow that didn't belong there.

My feet forgotten, I walked over the gravel and stepped onto the marshy grass of the field. Now that I was closer, I held the light up again.

Slowly, the weak beam illuminated what appeared to be a torso, a neck ... until finally reaching the eerie white glow of a face.

Chapter Eleven

I inched my way through the grass, toes sloshing in the ice-cold mud, too-tall grass nipping at my ankles.

There's another body in the field. In the exact same spot as Jenny...

My body burned with adrenaline, stomach doing somersaults in my throat, and the fear ... *the fear*. I should have felt it, but the same thing that compelled me to look all those years ago was driving me forward now. *Why can't I be one of those people who run?! Who look the other way...?*

I stopped ten feet from the body, eyes narrowing at the blank face, the mirrorless black eyes staring back at me...

It's not real. It's not real. It's not real.

So many years ago, I had wished—*prayed*—that the body in the field wasn't real. Then, my wish hadn't come true.

But this time ... *this time the outcome is different.*

Breathing a sigh of relief, I stepped forward, moving faster now and knelt beside the mannequin on the ground.

The face was blank, the head hairless, mouth in a strange O position. And there weren't even any arms or legs … *how did I miss that at first glance?*

I'd seen these stupid dolls before … during a CPR course I took as a teen when, once upon a time, I dreamed of working as a lifeguard at the local pool. The dolls were used to emulate choking or lifeless persons, and as I touched the cold plastic face, I remembered another version of me, down on my knees, trying to administer rescue breaths to my brother.

It's so easy to remember the number of breaths and chest compressions when you're sitting in a class getting drilled … but in that moment of panic, faced with my brother dead on the floor … my mind had drawn a blank.

I'd pounded on his chest, then pinched his nose and tried to breathe … *breathe, Jack. Dammit, BREATHE.*

But Jack was beyond breathing … even to the most untrained eye, there was no saving my brother.

Grimacing, I reached for the note. It was pinned to the front of the mannequin's chest:

If you help her, this will be you soon.

Stunned, I leapt to my feet, once again shining my light through the desolate field and illuminating the trees beyond.

That's when I saw them: two young girls, peeping out from either side of a fat oak tree. My breath froze in my chest. Because for a few seconds, I thought … *I thought they were Jenny and Chrissy, two ghosts watching me from the safety of the tree's shadowy embrace …*

"Hey!" I shouted into the darkness, my voice ricocheting through the trees.

What happened next wasn't planned … I have no memory of making the choice to chase them. But the next thing I knew, I was moving. Slipping and sliding through the thick brown mud, running after the girls…

"Get back here, you little brats!" I screamed. I darted through the trees, branches whipping across my face, catching in my hair … and my robe flying behind me like a madman's cape.

I slammed into the backside of one of the girls, knocking her to the ground and toppling headlong with her.

Dizzily, I used my scratched-up palms to lift myself off the girl. She was on her back now looking up at me, crab-crawling backwards away from me. Her eyes wide as saucers.

She's looking at me like I'm the boogeyman…

"Don't hurt us. It was only a joke!" whined the girl, her voice nasal and scared. Looking at her close up, it became apparent that she was only twelve or thirteen. *Just a baby.*

Another girl stepped out from between two trees. Her hair was long and dark brown, all the way to her waist. She had both hands on her hips. Unlike the other girl, she looked closer to being a woman than a child.

"Don't try anything," she warned. "The cops are already on their way."

She held up her cell phone triumphantly.

Chapter Twelve

"**T**heir parents are on their way to get them. What were you thinking ... chasing two young girls in the dark?"

I stared at Nash Winslow's face, still shaken by its familiarity.

I'd never had any run-ins with Officer Winslow before, but I felt like I'd seen him a thousand times ... over and over again in my memory. But it wasn't him in my memories—it was his father, working the case out there in the field.

"You look just like your dad," I said, softly. It was a strange response to his question, but I was still out of breath and shaken up. Seeing the spitting image of his father in my field had brought back so many memories, and not particularly good ones.

"Did you meet him when he worked the case?" Nash squinted his eyes at me.

I nodded, circling back to memories of his father. Hands on his hips like a cowboy from the Wild West, as he broke the news to my parents that the lumpy mass in the field was indeed a real human girl.

"You're lucky their parents don't want to press charges."

I was sitting on the front porch step of the farmhouse, ratty old robe wrapped tightly around me as I shivered and shook. I glanced over at the girls. They were huddled together at the edge of the field, tennis shoes slapping the edge of the gravel drive, as they waited for their parents to get here. The older one had given her jacket to the younger. They were shivering, the youngest girl's face snotty with tears. She had a few scrapes and bruises from our tussle, but nothing major.

"What about me, huh? They were trespassing. And they left that stupid note and dummy in … in the same place Jenny was… What was I supposed to think when I followed them? I didn't realize they were only kids. The note was threatening … did you read it?"

Nash sighed, then nodded. His hair was scruffy and brown like his father's, those same deep-set hazel eyes … and as much as I hated to admit it, as a young girl, I'd been attracted to the rough and tough policeman who visited our property dozens of times that year… *What would Nash think if he knew I'd had a crush on his late father?*

Looking into his son's face, my cheeks burned with embarrassment.

"You're right. They shouldn't have been here. What they did was wrong and I'm sure their parents will deal with them accordingly. Do you want to press charges?"

I glanced over at the girls, then shook my head.

"Who are they anyway? I've been back here for ten years and I've never seen them. Of course, I don't know many kids around here anymore..."

Nash's eyes settled back on me. "Amanda Butler and Cally Kells. Middle school students at Austin Junior. My guess is that this was some sort of dare, but they're not talking. I'm certain that they stole the dummy from a supply closet in the nursing station at school."

Cally looked young and frail, wispy white strands of hair stuck like glue to the corners of her mouth. Her eyes and nose were red—from the crying or the cold, I wasn't sure.

"I didn't mean to scare the girl, but I didn't know who was out there."

As though she had heard, the older girl—Amanda—raised her eyes to meet mine. There was something familiar about them—dark, determined, challenging...

If looks could kill, I thought drably.

"Dammit." Nash lifted his head to the wind, listening. There was a crow in the distance; it fluttered from one tree to the next with a warning caw.

"What?" I said, standing up. Still cinching closed my embarrassingly dirty robe.

The whir of engines in the distance.

"The parents?" I asked, leerily.

"Nah, the press. I'd bet money on it."

"Fuck me…" I looked over at the girls. Cally's weepy eyes were now wide and glistening. Amanda flashed a triumphant smile at me. Once again, I felt like I knew that face … those eyes, that smile…

"Who called—" But before I could finish my question, news vans were whipping into the gravel lot. The girls were on their feet now, both wearing innocent, wimpy expressions.

I rolled my eyes. "Do I have to stay out here?"

Nash's hands were on his hips as he glared at the reporters.

"Nah. Go on in."

But a young red-haired reporter was already out of the van, trying to flag me down as I pushed my way through the door.

I looked her straight in the face, my hair and face crazed I'm sure, and said, "They trespassed."

Back inside, I shivered from head to toe as I changed out of my robe and put on jeans and a heavy gray sweatshirt. A chill had settled over me; I couldn't warm up no matter how hard I tried, as though there were a block of ice settling over my bones.

Thirty minutes later, I was sitting at the kitchen table,

still shell-shocked, when there was a gentle knock at the door.

Tentatively, I crept to it and peeked out, making sure the press was gone.

They were, and so were the girls. Nash was standing on my front porch, looking weary.

"May I come in?" he asked, as I opened the door.

What choice do I have?

Sighing, I held the door open for him, eyes drifting down to the gun on his hip I hadn't noticed earlier. It wasn't strange—seeing a cop with a gun—but still… the sight of the weapon brought another surge… of what? *Fear?*

It felt like a symbol of violence to me, instead of a measure of protection. *Nothing feels safe in this town anymore, not that it ever did.*

I led him through the arched doorway of the living room and motioned for him to take a seat in the kitchen.

It was still early, barely 5am, but there was no going back to sleep now. I turned on my Keurig machine and popped a coffee pod inside.

"It's one cup at a time. Sorry," I said, sitting down across from him as the coffee maker gargled and hissed.

"I ran the press off. And the girls were picked up by their parents with no incident," Nash assured me. He looked around the kitchen and I could see it—curiosity.

"They were trespassing. I did nothing wrong." Images floated up of me running wildly through the woods, knocking down a child in the dark… I grimaced.

"You're right. They were in the wrong. And they had more to say when the parents showed. I was right. Just a prank. The school nurse will be happy to have her dummy returned. Those things are expensive."

"Hilarious prank." I stood up and went to the coffee maker. I removed the cup and started another.

I didn't have any children of my own—a decision I thought I might live to regret but never did—but if I had... they might be around Amanda or Cally's ages by now...

I sat the cup down in front of Nash, then offered him sugar and cream. He shook his head and blew steam off the top of the cup.

"Who are the parents? Anyone I know?" I asked.

"Amanda is Chuck and Adrianna Butler's daughter. Cally lives with her grandfather, Sal Newton. Know them?"

I groaned. "I don't know Sal. But Adrianna. Might that be Adrianna Montgomery, the columnist?"

But she was more than "the columnist" to me. She'd been my best friend, before she and her family decided to treat me and mine like lepers.

That line between friend and enemy stretched too thin between us...

"Yeah, the one and the only. I think she still uses her maiden name Montgomery in the papers."

"She sure does." I sighed, adding sugars and creamer to my cup. Then I took a long, hot sip, burning my tongue. "What did they have to say about what their daughters were doing?" Part of me wondered if Adrianna had put Amanda up to it, but no... that was too low, even for her.

"Honestly, they were embarrassed. I don't think they even realized the girls had snuck out. And they were furious with Amanda for taking the other girl. Cally is a few years younger, but they're neighbors and friends, you see..."

"Who called the press?"

Nash shrugged. "My guess is Amanda. Don't be surprised if your face pops up on Facebook after this. She told my dispatcher that you attacked them in the woods and she 'had proof'. She might have been filming or Facebook living for all we know..."

I closed my eyes and sighed deeply. I'd given up on social media years ago and I had no plan to get on there now, especially not with the recent news and ... now this.

"Why is everyone so angry with me? And why not go throw eggs at Chrissy's trailer or something? Why come here?" I wondered aloud.

"Because this is where it happened. This is the scary place." Nash did air quotes as he said "scary place".

"My family had nothing to do with Jenny's death," I said, bitterly.

"I know that. And my dad knew that too when he was alive. I was only five when it all happened, but I learned about it later... he talked about that case until his dying day."

That surprised me. "He did?"

Nash nodded.

"You know she's saying she's innocent," I said, quietly.

Nash abruptly chuckled into his cup. "And you know that's bull, right?"

I shrugged. "I mean, I don't believe everything she tells me, if that's what you're saying... but it's worth a listen, don't you think?"

I didn't tell him the truth—that I suspected there was something more, something his dad might have missed.

Nash's face hardened. "I don't think she deserves any sort of audience, to be honest with you. I mean, come on, why did she come back here? What was her reasoning? Have you bothered asking her that?"

My face warmed. "I have but I can't discuss our interviews right now. We've only met twice, so we're just getting started."

"You should talk to Katie," Nash said.

"Katie?" But I already knew who he meant. Katrina Juliott, Jenny's mother.

"She still live around here?" I asked, hesitantly. I thought about her son, Jenny's brother Mike, that I'd seen at the vigil the other night.

When Nash nodded, I asked, "Why in the world would Katie Juliott talk to me?"

Nash set his cup down slowly and ran his fingers through his shaggy hair. "Because, like you, she always wanted more. She had doubts about Chrissy's guilt, too."

Chapter Thirteen

T here is more than one way to kill a person. Not all of those ways involve death.

Katie Juliott wasn't dead and buried like her daughter Jenny. Nevertheless, she was still gone. *The lights are on but no one's home.*

There was something vacant in the old woman's eyes as she led me inside her house. She didn't act surprised when I showed up on her doorstep. She didn't ask who I was.

I hadn't seen her in years and years... *how could she possibly know who I am?*

She was wispy and thin. The full rosy cheeks I remembered from my childhood, that aristocratic nose and the way she held herself—always primly dressed and quiet —were gone.

Now Jenny's mom was skin and bones, her eyes vacant. Lost.

But there was beauty in the way she moved ... as though beauty and tragedy were intertwined, one impossible without the other...

"I was just cooking supper. Here's your plate, dear."

I was sitting on a bar stool at the breakfast counter, watching Jenny's frail mother move around the kitchen noiselessly, ghostlike.

Supper? It's barely noon.

And she still hadn't asked me what I was doing here... *Maybe she thinks I'm someone else. Maybe she doesn't know I'm interviewing her daughter's supposed murderer for a story.*

"Thank you," I said, as Katie slid a ceramic plate filled with food in front of me. The scent of tomato and cheese filled the room and my belly grumbled. There was a large square of lasagna on one side and a pile of chips and salsa on the other. A weird combination, but I didn't want to be rude, and truthfully, it all smelled delightful.

I plucked up a chip and dipped it in the thick red salsa.

"I made those chips myself," Katie said, proudly. She smiled for the first time, her face coming alive with it.

The chip was deliciously crisp and the salsa oddly sweet and savory. I closed my eyes, relishing the bite. I hadn't realized until this very moment... I'd been running on coffee and adrenaline for days.

Katie was still watching me, so I scooped up a hearty bite of lasagna. Unlike the salsa, the lasagna wasn't quite right—the noodles felt too hard, the meat slightly... raw.

As Katie turned toward the stove, I spit the hunk of beef

in my hand—it was cold and pink—and I slid it under a slippery noodle to hide it.

Is she trying to poison me?

But I knew that was a ridiculous thought. Nash had warned me, when I told him I might visit as suggested, that Katie had Alzheimer's and her lucidity came and went.

"Mrs. Juliott, I came to ask you a few questions about Jenny. Would that be all right?"

She was standing at the stove top, back turned to me, slowly scrubbing one of the burners with a rag. She stopped and turned, her eyes focusing in on mine for the first time since my arrival.

"You're going to write it, aren't you?"

The directness of her stare and question sent a nervous wave of nausea through my stomach.

"I'm not sure yet. I'm just hearing what she has to say. I don't see any reason to repeat what's already been said over the years. And I don't intend to cause any pain or discomfort for—"

Katie lifted one hand to stop me.

She walked over and looked at the plate in front of me, brow furrowing, then whisked it away before I could reach for another bite.

"Thank you for the food. It was delicious. I'm just not very hungry…" My belly rumbled noisily, betraying me.

Katie dropped the plate in the sink, food and all. I flinched at the ear-splitting clank.

"I have early-onset Alzheimer's. I almost wish I didn't

have these moments ... these moments when I realize what's happening."

"I'm so sorry," I mumbled, because I didn't know what else to say. She had to be ... I tried to do the math quickly. Katie was older than my mother back then ... so, she had to be around seventy now.

Her withdrawn face and fragile frame made her look older than seventy though.

"Wait right here. I want to show you something while my head is on straight."

As Katie wandered out of the room, I looked around the kitchen for any signs of Jenny. This was the house she grew up in, in a neighborhood much different than mine. The houses here were old but mid-sized with small backyards, your quintessential middle-class family.

As Katie returned, I rose to help her—she was carrying two heavy books that appeared to be photo albums. My heart fell at the sight of them.

I wasn't opposed to looking at photos of Jenny, but I'd seen a lot of her school pics online, and what I really wanted to discuss was Chrissy.

"Over here," Katie motioned, leading me to a large dining area adjacent to the kitchen.

The table was massive, enough to seat eight people. My thoughts fluttered back to Jenny's brother. *Does he still live here? And if so, how would he feel about me coming over, asking his sick mother questions?* I cringed at the thought, hoping Mike didn't show.

I took a seat beside Katie and watched her bird-like hands as they lifted the leather cover. The first photo was of Jenny. She was young, probably five or six in the photo. This wasn't one I'd seen before.

She was wearing a frilly white dress that summer, her stubby legs and feet ridiculously cute in her mother's heels. And to top it all off, there was a cowboy hat on her head, the bill so big it was hiding most of her eyes and nose. She looked so normal ... so happy.

Katie reached over to turn the page, and the next thing I knew I was getting flooded by a barrage of pictures—Jenny in a tiger swimsuit on the beach, tummy round and cheeks warm from the sun. Jenny with a fishing pole, standing next to an older boy with long, tan legs and matching hair. Jenny cradled in her mother's arms, chubby and soft as goo on the day she was born...

Seeing her this way filled me with an odd sensation. *A realization.* Jenny Juliott wasn't "the dead girl" or a case to be remembered ... she was a real girl. Someone's sister. Someone's daughter.

For the first time, I wondered—*really* wondered: *what did it feel like when it happened? Did she feel the life being sucked out of her second by second...? Did she see it coming? Did she know who her killer was? Was she staring in her killer's eyes before they fluttered shut for all time? And most importantly: was it Chrissy's eyes she saw that day when she took her final breath*?

Mostly I wondered: *Was she scared when she died?*

"I told her not to trust that girl," Katie said.

"Excuse me?"

Her finger shook as she stopped on a picture and pointed at one of two girls.

Jenny as a young child, hair wispy and white. Her smile wide, but full of missing teeth. And beside her ... those dark, mischievous eyes, that haunting smile ... *Chrissy*.

"I'm surprised they took a picture together. I didn't think they were really friends..." I said, shakily.

Katie surprised me by slamming the book shut and scooting it across the table. She reached over, grasping my hand ... her grip tighter than I would have imagined ... almost too tight.

"I told you that girl was trouble," she said.

I blinked, staring back at this woman who, once again, looked vacant and lonely inside.

"Who?" I asked, playing along.

"Chrissy, that's who. You should have taken John's word over hers. Those Cornwalls are nothing but liars and trash."

She thinks I'm Jenny.

Thoughts circled back to those letters in the shoe box—John, pursuing Chrissy. Jenny thanking her for telling the truth.

I'd heard many theories over the years, mostly on conspiracy threads on Reddit and overzealous crime bloggers ... but I'd never heard that Chrissy and Jenny were friends. In every theory, regardless of whodunnit, it was clear that Chrissy and Jenny were fighting over a boy.

"Why do you trust John so much?" I asked, tentatively.

John Bishop, no longer a boy. He was fat and balding, living two towns over with a wife and three kids. If only Chrissy and Jenny knew what a *prize* he'd really turn out to be…

It seemed wrong, pressing answers from a woman who might not give them to me willingly if she wasn't sick.

"It's obvious, isn't it?" Katie huffed. "He adores you, honey. He always has. Now that other boy, I don't trust him…"

"What other boy?"

"Don't play dumb with me, girl. I've seen the way your face lights up at the mention of his bloody name."

Who in the hell could she be talking about?

"I don't know who you mean," I said, honestly.

"Jack Breyas, of course. That boy and his family … they're good enough, but they don't go to church. He's not good enough for you either."

I gasped at the sound of my brother's name. *What did he have to do with Jenny? They were never an item, were they? He barely reacted at the news of her death … in fact, he was visiting Aunt Lane when it happened … he didn't even attend Jenny's funeral…*

Suddenly, the walls felt too narrowing, too tight. My breath lodged in my throat, I choked out the words, "I have to go, Mrs. Juliott. Thanks for the lovely meal."

She raised her eyebrows at me, then surprised me by saying, "Okay, let me walk you out."

At the door, she placed her hand on my arm. I was so shaken, it made me freeze in place.

"Do you feel her there ... her presence still around on the farm?"

Does she remember who I am again now? I wondered, exasperated.

"Who do you mean?" I stammered.

"My Jenny. Is she still there? Do you feel her with you sometimes?"

Her words, spoken so softly and with such hopefulness, sent a wave of sadness through me.

"Not really. But I think that's because she didn't die there, Mrs. Juliott. Her body was there, yes, but I don't think it was where she was murdered..."

The look on Katie's face was devastating.

Quickly, I added, "But I think about her all the time, so maybe she is there. I don't know."

"And your brother? Do you feel him too?"

I shuddered and shook my head, letting myself out without another word.

Did Jack know more about Jenny's death than he'd let on? And is that why he eventually committed suicide all those years ago?

Chapter Fourteen

I found him on a Friday night. *It was ten years ago but, in truth, it feels like only yesterday.*

The radio was on in the kitchen, one of those old-timey things attached below the cabinets. It was playing at full volume, just like old times when Mom was still there. She loved to read or listen to music while she cooked our supper, sometimes both.

I smiled when I walked in, a pleasant sense of being home settling over me for the first time in years.

The kitchen was empty, and yet ... I could still see her standing there. In her summer tank tops and old blue jeans; she never wore shorts, not even in the dog days of summer.

I missed her smile and I missed her food. I missed hearing the music of my childhood ... a summer soundtrack I'd never forget ... the flipping pages of her books and the low hum of her off-key voice as she sang along to all the songs she knew…

For a while, she seemed so happy. But then after Jenny died, her relationship with Dad unraveled … and suddenly, she no longer wanted to stay. There were rumors—drugs, another man, a mental breakdown—but I think she just got sick of being our mother, frankly.

"Jack! Where you at?" I called.

I followed the sounds of something else, leaving the music behind … it was the swishing of the fan upstairs. Just like it always had, the fan still rocked and swayed when turned on full speed, threatening to rip itself from the ceiling…

I climbed the steps, two at a time. Eager to see my brother.

He'd asked me to come a dozen times—first, to live with him, and when that didn't work, he asked me constantly to come visit. My decision to come was spur of the moment … I was hoping to surprise him and seeing his truck out front had made me smile.

I just hope he doesn't have a girl up there, I thought, grimly.

"Jack?"

As I reached the top of the stairs, I could see that he was in his room. The light was on and his door was open. Despite taking over the farm after Daddy's heart attack, he hadn't switched his room to the master. It seemed childish —staying in his old room all this time.

I stepped into the doorway, smiling big ... all my molars showing. But my temporary glee melted instantly.

Because this wasn't how I expected to find him.

'Sweet and Low' by Augustana was playing on the radio downstairs. *I'll never forget that song.* Dad's old shotgun lay next to him on the floor.

I fell to the floor beside him, trying to resuscitate him ... although I knew. I *knew* he was gone long before I'd arrived.

Because at the top of his head, that messy tuft of hair I used to tug on, was a hole so big that I could have fit my fist inside it.

Chapter Fifteen

As I slammed the door of the car and wedged the shifter in gear, I couldn't get my mind off Jack. Off that night, ten years ago ... when all my future plans changed. When I lost the only family I had left. And the way he did it ... that jagged red hole at the top of his skull, bits of bone and brain matter splattered on the carpet and walls...

I thought about my "office" now, the slick gray coat of paint, the furniture replaced, the carpet removed and restored to its original pine heart flooring ... but it was still Jack's room. It would always be his room. The room he laid his head in for all those years; and the room where he blew it apart.

He left no note. No explanation. Not even a clue on his mobile or email accounts.

Why didn't he call me? Why didn't he reach out for help?

But that nasty, unforgiving voice inside me reminded me as it always did: *maybe he wouldn't have done it if you'd hadn't moved away. Or if you'd gone to visit more often…*

Jack had struggled with depression. That was no secret. But I had depression, too. *When does the line between depression cross into complete desperation, with no will to live?*

But then that voice again: *Don't pretend you haven't considered it either.*

After he died, I thought I wouldn't be able to stay. The farm was mine, after all. Mom out there living her new life and Dad dead and buried in the ground. There was no one left to take it but me after Jack died.

But instead of being unable to stay, I found that I could not leave.

I felt, somehow, that I owed it to Jack to be there.

Did you know something about Jenny's death? Is that why you did it? Or was it just too depressing to be in that house, after losing Dad and Mom leaving, and the tragedy that occurred there, Jack…?

Oh, what I wouldn't give for a chance to ask him all those questions now.

I'd gotten rid of Dad's guns and had the room cleaned and redone. I'd tried to whisk away the bad memories of his suicide and hold onto the ones before … the ones of us as children. We were close, almost too close, in that way some siblings are. We could get along better than anyone, but at the same time … we could go from zero to sixty and be at each other's throats for the dumbest things.

Oh, how I wish I could change it, Jack.

All the games—the hide and seek, the make-believe worlds we'd created, the treasures we'd looked for—those were the good times. *The times I want to hold on to.* But, in my mind, I still saw what he looked like there on the floor … I could never forget that version of him. *The broken brother I couldn't save.*

I couldn't face the bustle of in-town traffic, or the prospect of driving by Kmart. But I couldn't go home either … I wasn't ready to return to my empty tomb just yet.

Residential homes faded away, the familiar fields returning and blurring by in my periphery. Trees, so many trees … *there were so many places the killer could have dumped Jenny's body. Why the farm? And why did Katie Juliott mention my brother? Was she simply confused…? Mixing up my brother with John Bishop?*

Of course Jack knew Jenny. They went to school together.

But, as far as I knew, Jack ran around in different circles —band members and goth kids and the quiet ones. Those were Jack's people.

And he hadn't even been in Austin when Jenny died. When he'd returned and heard the news of Jenny's death, he hadn't seemed upset. Just shocked, like the rest of us.

I didn't realize where I was going until I made a sharp right on Wilson Lane then a left on Willow Run. *I have to talk to Chrissy. I need to ask her what she knows about Jack…*

Dennis's truck was parked in the driveway, impulsively

crooked, like he'd turned up in a hurry. As I parked directly behind him, I was thankful the press was gone. *Are they finally getting bored with this? I hope so*, I thought, dully.

Showing up uninvited at Dennis's trailer was risky at worst, rude at best. *But it's not like Chrissy hadn't done the same thing to me a few days ago...*

I left my satchel on the passenger's seat and turned the engine off. Slowly, I approached the trailer. It was two in the afternoon; too late for most people to be sleeping, but Chrissy had said Dennis worked third shift.

I'd barely made it to the porch ramp when I heard the sound of glass breaking, coming from inside the trailer.

"Oh, fuck you, Dennis! Keep your damn hands off me. I mean it!"

I froze, my foot resting on the first porch step. *Should I call the police, or just leave?*

"What are ya gonna do? Call the cops, bitch? They'd probably come in and whack ya themselves," Dennis screamed.

There was a loud thump and a muffled cry, followed by the sounds of grunts and groans inside.

I darted up the rest of the steps, banging both my fists on the screen door.

Immediately, things on the other side of the door grew quiet.

I banged again, with one fist now. "It's Natalie Breyas. I'm here to pick up Chrissy for our interview."

Seconds later, the door swung open, nearly knocking me off the thin stamp of porch.

Dennis's face was red and blotchy, his eyes wide as saucers. He huffed from his nose like a caged bull, then said, "Good, please get her out of here."

For a moment, I was scared he would ask me in. But then Chrissy's face appeared behind him. Her nose and mouth were bleeding.

For the first time since meeting her in person, she looked as defeated as she had on camera following her release from prison.

"Come on," I said, motioning her to come with me. Dennis was glaring at me, still breathing hard, but I couldn't manage to raise my eyes to meet his.

I wasn't exactly frightened of him; I had my cell phone in my pocket and could call the cops if I needed to. But I was afraid of doing anything to set him off; anything to give him a reason not to let her leave.

Chrissy coughed in her hand, using the opportunity to swipe at the blood on her face.

"I forgot about our meeting. Let me grab a few things and I'll meet you out there in a minute."

The last thing I wanted to do was let Dennis close the door and for her to disappear back inside that trailer ... *but what choice did I have?*

I got back in my car and waited. Minutes passed, my heart beating in my chest like a drum. I clenched my hands into tight fists, nails digging into my palms.

I could remember Mom and Dad fighting, angry voices behind their door. Dad had never hit her, but they'd argued viciously when they thought they were "alone". It was no surprise when she left us. I was only fourteen when she went. She took everything with her ... her clothes and shoes, all of her jewelry. *Every piece of her was gone, almost like she'd never been there in the first place.*

The fallout and stress after the Juliott murder tipped her over the edge.

But I wish she would have taken me with her. She wasn't the only one who wanted to escape Austin...

"I have to go away soon," she had told me. "I want you to know that I love you. Me leaving ... it has nothing to do with you. Your dad and I ... and what happened to that girl ... I just can't stay here anymore." She warned us so many times she was going, but I didn't think she really would.

I was almost ready to get back out and approach the trailer, when the front door banged open and shut. Chrissy emerged from the rickety porch, a ratty old backpack slung over her left shoulder.

If she leaves Dennis, where will she go? I wondered.

As Chrissy folded herself into my car's passenger seat, I released a pent-up whoosh of breath.

I guess we'll cross that bridge when we get to it, I decided.

I clicked the automatic locks and backed away from the grimy old trailer.

We were sitting in my den like two girlfriends, paper plates filled with thick, gooey slices of pizza balanced on both of our laps.

"I haven't had pizza in years," Chrissy moaned, closing her eyes as she chewed an oversized bite of sausage and pepperoni.

The traces of blood were gone; she'd barely mentioned the incident with Dennis since getting in the car with me. Her stomach was rumbling and so was mine after that messy meal at Katie's. I'd considered stopping somewhere to eat, but I didn't want to draw any attention to us.

"Where is this from again?" Chrissy asked, finishing off one piece and promptly scooping up another from the box.

"Gia's. It's been around for a while, but not since..."

"Not since I went to prison," Chrissy finished for me.

I nodded. I'd gone outside to meet the delivery boy, leaving Chrissy in the house so she wasn't spotted. With no vehicle to place her here, I was hoping the news vans would stay away.

"I heard about what happened last night," Chrissy said, talking through a mouth full of cheese and sauce.

My stomach turned, remembering the incident with the girls. Specifically, Adrianna's daughter.

"How did you hear about that?" I dropped my pizza plate on the floor by my feet, then sank deeper in the cushions, head swimming with exhaustion. I'd barely slept in the last twenty-four hours, but it was more than that—I felt mentally drained by it all.

"Facebook, where else? There's a private group on there, discussing my homecoming. Local peeps," she added, as I raised my eyebrows.

"If it's private, how do you know about it?"

"Well, I don't know ... I don't understand how this social media stuff works. I could see the group, but I couldn't see the posts. So, naturally, I infiltrated."

For some reason, that didn't surprise me. It sounded like something I'd do, if I wanted to sneakily get information.

"What did they say about last night?"

"Just that some local teens put a plastic dummy in the field." Chrissy smirked at me.

"And? What else did they say?" I asked, rubbing my eyes drearily.

"That you chased them like a banshee through the woods in your bathrobe."

I rolled my eyes. "Jesus. Let me guess? Adrianna's in the Facebook group."

"Yeah. I think so. But who cares?" Chrissy shrugged. She picked up her cup of soda and chugged it loudly.

I winced as she burped in my direction.

"Sorry. Prison isn't exactly charm school," she teased.

"So what happened back there with Dennis? You still haven't told me."

Chrissy's face hardened. "He's an asshole. I met him while I was in prison, through letters and calls. He's the brother of one of my fellow inmates. *Former* fellow inmate," she corrected.

"Why him? And who was this other inmate? How did you know her?" I pushed.

Part of me wanted to test her, to see if she'd lie about Alison Alinsky.

"His sister Alison was in prison with me. She was a real piece of work. Killed her own kid." Reading my mind, she added, "If I sound heartless, I'm sorry. We had to be that way ... to survive with all those awful people. Did you see this?" She pointed at the scar on her cheek.

"How did you get it?"

"Let's just say that kid killers aren't very popular in prison. I didn't even know the girl who cut me. It was my fourth year there when it happened, my face split open like a cantaloupe..."

Chrissy shuddered at the memory and I flinched.

"So, I guess I felt bad for Alison. She was quiet as a mouse, and I knew she'd get trampled over."

"So, when did you fall in love with her brother? How did that come about?" I asked.

Chrissy snorted. "I didn't fall in love with Dennis. Hell, I barely even like the guy. And that's the problem in his eyes, I guess. He always wanted more."

She went on, "He reached out to me in prison. His sister gave him my information. He wanted me to protect her, keep his little sister safe..."

"And did you?"

Chrissy grinned, her scar glowing in the shadowy living

room. "I promised to keep her safe and watch her back if he did me some favors too."

"What sort of favors?" I asked, reaching down for my coke. I was parched, my throat sore from screaming across the field last night.

"Well, she was severely mentally ill. I know the papers didn't make it out that way, but she truly was."

"Anyone who kills little kids is sick, I don't think anyone is doubting that," I said.

"Agreed. But Alison was delusional, and she heard voices. And she had trouble getting her anti-psychotics in prison. I helped smuggle them in through her brother, and I watched her back. We kid killers have to stick together," she said, bitterly.

"How long has he been abusing you?"

Chrissy froze. Slowly, she said, "I didn't know things would turn out this way. I thought I made it clear to him that I wasn't interested in a romantic or sexual relationship. He agreed to help me get a place or set up a place for us to stay temporarily until I could get a job and get on my feet. That was the deal. I had to have somewhere to live, as a condition of my parole, and his little sister needed help. I thought we understood each other."

"And that brings us back to the question: why here, Chrissy? Why return to Austin? You must know that getting a job in this town is going to be difficult." I know my words must have sounded harsh, but they were true. Chrissy had no future in this town; surely, she must have known that.

"I have no plans of staying here. I wanted to come back for a couple weeks and connect with my brothers, then maybe head west and try to find a waitressing job."

This is news to me.

"Your brothers? But surely you must have known they were gone."

Chrissy shrugged. "Like I said, I refused their calls and visits for years. And by the time I wanted them back around, they'd moved on with their lives. Their numbers had been changed…"

"Your older brother is in prison in Georgia. Drug crimes, I think. And I'm not sure about your younger brother. I know he and your parents moved away shortly after your conviction. I'm sorry," I said, softly.

Chrissy smiled, sadly. "I knew my parents left, but I guess I was still hoping Trevor might be around. I didn't realize he was serving time at the same time I was… I'm going to write him, but I haven't yet."

"But beyond that, what else is here for you? You know the townspeople will never forget you're here. They'll harass you till your dying day." Again, my words sounded harsher than I wanted them to. *But if I couldn't be honest, then what was the point? It made no sense for her to be here, and I wanted to understand WHY.*

But Chrissy was ready to talk about Dennis now.

"The first time he hit me was my third night in the trailer. I guess he was pissed when he realized there weren't going to be any perks of having me as a roommate." Her mouth twisted into an O of disgust. She reached for her soda again, but then changed her mind. "I was going to take off the next morning, maybe try to hitch a ride at the truck stop in Newbury, make my way along with the little money I had in my pocket from Dennis. But then, I woke up that morning and I found your letter in my mailbox. It felt like destiny, as cheesy as that might sound to you."

Destiny.

Such a strange thought ... but how many times had I thought about this case? Lost sleep as I read through the dark web chat rooms and the wild theories that made no sense over the years? I'd wanted to write this story for so long ... but now that she was here in front of me, I wasn't sure how to get to the truth.

"Well, if you want me to write this story, then you need to let me ask you some questions. I feel like all I know so far is mostly what I've already heard. Can you do that for me?"

Chrissy stood up and grabbed her backpack off the lazy-boy chair. She unzipped it and pulled out two cans of Monster energy drinks.

"I got hooked on these in prison, what can I say?" She laughed, then popped the top on one can and handed me the other. "You ready to stay up late and do this interview? I'll try to be more forthright this time."

I accepted the can and gave her a wary smile.

Is she planning to stay the night here? I wondered. The thought of her sleeping inside my house made me a little uneasy.

"Okay. Let's do it," I said.

"That chess board over there…" Chrissy pointed at my father's old chessboard, the one I kept on a small end table in the corner. It was a beautiful old set—black and white leather top with stone carved pieces. I used to grip them in my hands, rolling them back and forth, back and forth, when I was a child…

"Yeah?"

"Can we talk and play at the same time? I haven't played since I was a little girl. I miss it."

I miss it too, I wanted to say. But I didn't.

There were some quiet nights, alone in the farmhouse, when I played the game by myself. Moving around pieces on the board, my only opponent myself, and the ghosts of my father and brother in the room with me.

"You play chess?" I asked, trying to hide my surprise. Even I couldn't play much when I was younger. It wasn't until I was a teenager that Jack taught me the rules.

Chrissy rolled her eyes. "The Cornwalls might be trash, but we aren't stupid."

"I've never thought you were stupid, that's for sure," I assured her.

There were three light taps on the front door.

I stood and went to the window, peeking out through the blinds. For some reason, I'd been expecting the press or Dennis. But it was Officer Nash Winslow outside.

"It's the police. Can you go somewhere? I don't want to

give them any reason to stick around longer than they have to."

"What are they doing here?" Chrissy whispered.

"Probably following up on what happened last night."

I watched Chrissy disappear through the kitchen. She took a left down the hallway and went inside the bathroom.

I opened the front door and stepped outside.

"Hi, Nash," I said, stifling a legitimate yawn. That energy drink wasn't giving me much energy, at least not yet. "What can I do for you?"

Sheepishly, Nash held up a thick manilla folder.

I pulled the front door slightly closed behind me. "What's that?"

"My father's old case file. Or what I could find, anyway. I thought you might like to take a look. I'll need it back soon though," he said.

"Why are you doing this?" I said, plucking the folder from his hands before he could change his mind.

"Because you said she's claiming innocence. And if you've agreed to write her story, then I'm inclined to think you might believe her. Read those. Then tell me what you think."

"Thank you."

He seemed disappointed when I didn't invite him in, but finally, he waved and walked back to his cruiser.

Back inside, I quick-stepped down the hallway and closed myself in my bedroom. I heard the bathroom door open. "Is he gone?" Chrissy called through the hallway.

"Yeah. He was just checking in. I'm changing my shirt. Be out in a minute. Why don't you go ahead and set up the chess board?"

"Okay," Chrissy said, her voice eager and enthusiastic.

I stared down at the thick old file in my hands, wishing I could read it now. But first, I needed to talk to Chrissy and find out what her next steps were and try to get in as many questions as she would allow.

I slid the folder between my mattress and box spring for later.

Chapter Sixteen

I expected Chrissy to be an aggressive chess player. But she surprised me, taking out her pawns early. Letting me take the lead.

I had both knights in play, a clear path to move my bishop. But, somehow, I felt leery of her cool and collected approach to the game.

"I went to see Katrina Juliott today." I took out one of Chrissy's pawns, sacrificing my own. But Chrissy didn't take the bait, not with the pawn or my statement. I'd expected a reaction from her, but her face was blank, unreadable.

"She has Alzheimer's. For a while, she thought I was Jenny," I said.

Chrissy grimaced at the dead girl's name.

"And she showed me pictures ... one was of you and Jenny. That was quite a surprise."

Finally, Chrissy slid one of her bishops out. But before she removed her fingers from the piece, she slid it back to its rightful place, choosing another pawn instead.

"I'm not surprised. I told you we knew each other. You read the letters in the shoebox I gave you?" Chrissy asked, eyes never leaving the board.

"I did." I made no more moves, sitting back in my chair and focusing on Chrissy's face. After the energy drinks, I'd made glasses of Jack and Coke. Jack and soda for her, only Coke for me. I needed to loosen her up. Needed to get some answers. My head and heart were too heavy for drinking tonight.

"This picture I saw … you both looked younger, maybe only eight or nine when it was taken."

"We knew each other before John Bishop. We went to elementary school together for several years," Chrissy said.

"I thought you were homeschooled," I breathed.

Chrissy shook her head. "That began in middle school. My parents saw the paths my brothers were headed down and they felt like I'd be better at home with them. Of course, Dad was rarely there. But my mom taught me. She wasn't the greatest teacher, but she made me do the work. She wasn't lazy and incompetent like the stories would have you believe," Chrissy said. Then she added, "It's your move, by the way."

I slid one of my castles across the board, facing down one of her pawns. I'd always had a preference for the castle piece—its versality and strength.

"Why does Jenny's mom have a photo of you two? Were you friends before you switched to the homeschooling track?" I asked.

Chrissy sighed. "I don't know if you'd call us friends. We were in the same class in third grade. She invited me over a few times, that was all. I don't think her parents were crazy about her hanging out with a Cornwall, to be honest."

"Why do you say that?" I asked.

"Because they were rich and pretty, and my family was ugly and poor, why else? It was easy to forget about us, to underestimate us…"

I'd forgotten about the bishop. She slid it across the board, taking down my castle in one swell swoop.

"Let's talk about that day. You didn't have your driver's license, but you supposedly forced Jenny inside your brother's truck. You took her somewhere and killed her, then you dumped her body in our field. If you didn't want her boyfriend and she used to kind of be your friend, then why? Why would you admit to all that?" I asked, boldly.

Chrissy's jaw flexed in her cheek, then she reached for her drink. I watched as she drained the whiskey.

"Can I have another one?" Chrissy slid her glass toward me, not waiting for an answer.

"Sure. But then will you tell me about that day … the true story?"

Chrissy grunted a word that might have been 'yes', eyeballing the pieces still left on the board.

It's time to take out my queen. I moved her out, then went to the kitchen to fetch Chrissy's drink.

This time I made the drink stronger. Chrissy needed it after her tussle with Dennis, and I needed her to trust me more. I filled another glass of Coke for me, then added a splash of whiskey.

"Here you go," I said, returning to the room.

Chrissy took a long swallow of her fresh drink.

She focused on the same bishop again. As she sat her glass down, her hand was wobbly, her limbs lanky and loose from the booze, and a bit of it swished over the side of her glass. She wiped it with the sleeve of her gray hoodie, then moved her bishop a single space.

Clearing her throat, she said, "I picked her up from school that day, that much was true. But I didn't force her. I didn't like her boyfriend ... but I must admit, I was flattered by his interest in me. And intrigued at first. But then I started to notice the way he was, and I felt like I should tell her. She deserved to know the truth about John."

"Okay..." I nodded slowly, urging her on. I wasn't taking notes this time. How could I forget her words? I couldn't. And I certainly didn't need paper or a tape recorder to absorb them.

"When I told her the truth, about him pursuing me, I thought she'd be angry with me, or maybe even deny it. You know how some girls are ... they don't want to accept the truth about the men they love..."

I nodded. "But John wasn't a man, Chrissy. He was a teenage boy."

Chrissy shrugged one shoulder. "He was. But you have to remember, we were young too. Full of hormones and full of rage…"

"Murdering someone takes a lot of rage," I said, solemnly.

Chrissy sighed dramatically. "Anyway, I picked her up that day. We didn't go anywhere. We just rode around and talked, and we smoked some pot I stole from Trent. She wasn't used to smoking … and by the time I dropped her off, she was more than a little high. I felt terrible about it honestly. I shouldn't have left her that way."

I wanted to believe her, but something was still missing here.

"She didn't make it home though, Chrissy. You say you dropped her off, but nobody saw her after that. The next time anyone saw her … she was lying dead in the field. And you confessed to the police that you were responsible. If it wasn't you, who was it? And why confess?"

Chrissy used her bishop to take out my knight, then drained her second glass. She slammed it hard on the table.

"Jenny's parents were strict as hell. Her daddy was a pastor, for Christ's sake. How do you think they would have reacted if she came home high, dropped off by a Cornwall with no license, no less? I couldn't drive her home that day." Chrissy's words were softly slurred.

I moved my knight, then she moved hers too. I had no

choice but to back off from her, in the game and in this conversation. She was getting visibly upset, flexing her jaw again.

But instead of retreating, I moved my queen, taking down one of her pawns.

Chrissy stared at the board, eyebrows furrowing.

"If you didn't drop Jenny off at home that night, then how did you both part ways?" I asked, keeping my voice even.

"I dropped her off at the park beside her neighborhood. You know, the one with the merry-go-round...?"

"I know the one." Although the merry-go-round had been gone for more than a decade. Too dangerous, according to the all the helicopter parents in Austin.

"She insisted on it. But truthfully, I was tired and high, and I didn't fight her on it. When I left her there, she was walking through the grass, headed toward the goldfish pond..."

But there was one huge problem with Chrissy's new story. "You told the cops you killed her. If your story is true, then you would never have done that. No one in their right mind confesses to a murder they didn't do..."

"Who said I was in my right mind?" Chrissy's eyes hardened, two shiny black marbles in the dark. She made another move, but I couldn't pull my eyes from her face.

"Why did you tell them you did it, Chrissy?"

"Because I was protecting someone. Checkmate."

I froze, a trickle of fear flowing through me. *Protecting who?*

When I looked down, my king was surrounded on all sides; either way I moved, I was dead.

"I had no more moves, don't you see? If I told the truth, my life was over. If I lied, it was over too," Chrissy slurred.

"Who were you protecting, Chrissy?"

Chrissy stared at my king, eyes watery and strange. "I used to sneak out of the trailer every night. Wander the dark roads sometimes, but mostly, I went down to the woods. I liked to sit by the creek, smoking. Thinking. I didn't see who put her in the field, but I saw her there before anyone else. I stood over her body. I cried beside her. Then I got scared and went back home. And you know what happens next."

Shakily, I moved my king, letting her castle take me.

"My parents found her. I saw her body from my brother's window," I said.

"And in the days that followed, there were all sorts of crazy theories… Do you remember that part too?" Chrissy asked.

I nodded.

But, truly, I didn't. I was young then. I knew my parents were shook up and the kids at school were talking … but I didn't really understand most of it until I was older.

"Someone at the school saw her with me that day, whipping out of the school parking lot. I didn't force her in the truck. Jenny wasn't scared of me! Did you read the letter she wrote me?"

I nodded. "I did. The letter with the initials 'JJ'."

Chrissy lifted her glass to her lips, sniffed at the empty tumbler then set it back down. She stared at the board, admiring her win.

"How did she end up in the field after you dropped her at the park, Chrissy?"

Chrissy shrugged. "She walked there, I guess. But someone stopped her. Someone…"

"Who?" I pressed. "Who were you protecting?"

"I've had too much to drink," Chrissy said, abruptly. She pushed back her chair and stood up, stumbling forward into the table. Chess pieces fell over, a couple hitting the soft carpet below.

"Can I stay here tonight? I know it's rude to ask, but I've had too much to drink and I'm not supposed to be drinking … plus, I can't go home to that … well, it's not even really my home. I don't have a fucking home anymore," she said, bitterly.

As much as I wanted to know the truth, she was too drunk to push right now.

"Okay, Chrissy. It's okay. You can sleep in my old room." I took her by the elbow, leading her toward the stairs.

Chrissy was clumsy, leaning hard into my shoulder, as we made our way up the stairs.

"If you want me to write this story, Chrissy, then I need to know who you were protecting. Who you're still protecting," I said, leading her to the door. "You can trust me. I'm on your side here."

"She was out there in the field, bugs crawling over her skin … worms eating her eyes. I can't stop thinking about it. How scared she must have been … how awful I was for not protecting her," she slurred.

Chrissy was choking up with tears now. I pushed her the rest of the way up the steps, keeping her steady as she took one step after another toward my childhood bedroom. My old bed was still in there, with the gold frame and itchy blue blankets.

She stumbled through the doorway and plopped face first on my bed, groaning.

"I don't feel good," she mumbled into the pillows, closing her eyes.

She still had her shoes on; the bed still neatly made beneath her body.

"Who were you protecting, Chrissy?" I asked again, softly in the dark.

But she was out like a light and I felt myself sigh in frustration. Gently, I rolled her into the recovery position, just in case. Then I closed the door, giving her privacy.

Chapter Seventeen

I closed the door to my bedroom, balancing a slice of cold pizza as I made my way for the bed. The files of the late Burt Winslow were stuffed between my mattress and box spring, beckoning me to read them.

Nibbling the pizza, I opened the worn-out folder; it was thick, nearly fifty sheets to go through, and I had no idea how long I'd have them. For all I knew, Nash might show up in the morning and whisk them away.

My mind circled back to Chrissy's last words.

Who was she protecting?

John Bishop? Her brothers? Or perhaps her father...

I tried to consider my own family: would I go down for a crime to protect them? I no longer had a family to protect; those who were living, out there somewhere, my mom and Aunt Lane, didn't matter. *They don't keep in touch, so why should I?*

If I knew Jack killed someone, would I take the fall?

I suppose it would depend on the circumstances...

Why is Chrissy being so vague? Why doesn't she come right out and say it? And if someone else really was involved in Jenny's death, what will the repercussions be for telling this story?

I thought about her chess strategy ... slow and methodical, a sneak attack from all sides...

Setting aside thoughts of our conversation, I removed the first ten pages from the file and spread them across my bed like a fan.

Nash's father may have been gone from this earth, but his stern voice spoke to me from the pages...

The probable cause affidavit, charging Chrissy with first-degree murder was page number one. A small trophy for him.

The report was mechanical and matter-of-fact, the justification for arresting Chrissy on July 15, 1981.

The most damning piece of evidence was her written confession. I pulled the rest of the sheets from the files, locating a copy of it—Chrissy's messy, childlike writing. I set it aside to read later.

There was more listed in the affidavit ... a muddy shoe print in the field, with a distinct converse emblem imprinted into the bottom. And then the straw that broke the camel's back: a pair of matching, filthy shoes photographed inside Chrissy's trailer. Specifically, in Chrissy's bedroom closet.

I flipped through the dusty old pages, looking for an image of the shoe print and the matching pair photographed at Chrissy's. I stopped, scalp prickling with fear, as I reached the glossy crime scene photos.

How many times have I seen her face ... eye bulging, her cheeks and lips bloated...?

But here they were, in full color, triggering a wave of memory and fear. My stomached twisted in knots, I fought the urge to vomit as I had all those years ago...

There were five photos in all. I pushed aside the other papers, lining up the photos in front of me. I forced myself to stare at her face, to study the wounds on her body.

The person who did this had been enraged.

Finally, unable to look for one more second, I turned them over, face down on my bed.

No matter—I could still see her, the image of her pain, the horrible suffering she must have endured burned on the back of my retinas for all eternity...

I went back to searching for the shoes. I found the photograph near the bottom of the stack. A muddy pair of sneakers tossed in the back of Chrissy's closet. A perfect match in the field. As I stared at the print and shoe side by side, I couldn't shake off Chrissy's altered version of events...

If she really went out to the field and saw the body, then ran back home in a rush ... then the print and shoes meant nothing. They only supported her claim that she was there and that she'd tossed them aside in a hurry, like she told me.

If she were the killer, wouldn't she have disposed of the shoes in the days following the murder? They weren't discovered until after her confession. Between the time of the murder and the confession, she'd made no effort to get rid of them ... besides tossing them in her closet.

But she had been barely a teenager. Maybe she just didn't think it through. Or perhaps, she had plans of confessing all along, and that's why she didn't hide them.

I allowed myself to consider Chrissy's story ... the new one she had given tonight.

The medical examiner had determined that Jenny wasn't killed in the field. She'd been dead before she got there.

I scanned through the brief typed report made by the medical examiner, Dr. Samantha Green.

There were thirteen stab wounds. Minor burns on her face and hands. Evidence of strangulation. She technically died of shock, blood loss, and then organ failure.

I shivered, closing my eyes. Fighting off the flashing images of that eye, of the deep, violent wounds on her back and belly.

I turned over one of the photos and examined her hands. There were some defensive wounds.

Which means she tried to fight off her killer...

Whose face did Jenny see on that cold dark night? Was it Chrissy's? Or someone else's...?

I didn't realize I was crying until I saw the drops of

water on the photo. Quickly, I used my thick black quilt to wipe it away.

Lying back on the bed, I swiped at my face. I was emotional, not to mention exhausted.

The clock on my nightstand read 3:33am.

The half-eaten pizza was still on the bed. Groaning, I set the plate on the nightstand, then pushed it as far away from me as possible.

The park near Jenny's home was less than a mile away. *Maybe she was coming this way to see Chrissy again—but why? Why did she suddenly need to come back to the girl? And who stopped her along the way?*

Someone who possibly wanted to frame Chrissy. Someone who also had a reason to hate Jenny. There was only one person who came to mind: *John Bishop*.

But John Bishop was supposedly cleared from the get-go —he was at football camp when the murder occurred.

Chrissy said she didn't force Jenny to go with her; that it was a friendly ride ... but if that were true, why did a witness say otherwise?

As far as I knew, the witness at the school had never been mentioned in the news or online. The claim itself had been exaggerated into: "Students at the school saw Chrissy force Jenny into her truck."

But that wasn't true. As I flipped over the next page, I found only one witness's statement in regard to the day Jenny left the school.

It wasn't another teenager from Austin middle, but a

third grader at Austin Elementary, in the adjacent playground, who had seen the incident between the two girls.

A student who'd stayed behind after school, waiting for her mother to pick her up … she'd seen the incident and told the police she was scared. I gasped as I read the witness's name: Adrianna Montgomery.

Carefully, I stacked the fragile photos and papers and slid them back inside their folder.

It was late and my eyes were heavy with sleep. *I'll go through this more in the morning*, I decided, closing my eyes and letting this new revelation about Adrianna sink in. We had been friends then, the best of friends … *why didn't she tell me about it?*

I tucked the folder under my mattress again and crawled beneath the covers. For the first time in a long time, I imagined my parents in this room.

And the room above me … the place where I used to lay my head. *There's a possible killer up there now*, I thought with a shiver.

I turned out my lamp, but I couldn't close my eyes. Above me, I stared at the swirling popcorn patterns on the ceiling, imagining Chrissy in my old bed.

My bedroom door was locked tight. But still … the thought of her being so close, in my house, in my room … made my stomach twist with unease.

If she did kill Jenny, then there's an evil person lying above me.

She might be lying.

But did I really believe that? *No,* I decided. *There's a reason this case has always bothered me ... and I need to know who Chrissy was protecting if I want the truth.*

Chapter Eighteen

I woke up shivering, bladder full, and my head throbbing from crying myself to sleep. As I opened my eyes, the first things I noticed were the shadows on my bedroom walls.

It's not morning. It can't be.

Groaning, I glanced over at the alarm clock. 5am. I'd been asleep for a little over an hour…

That's when I heard it, the dull metallic bang from below. I jerked up in bed, panting. *What was that?*

There was another bang, followed by a series of rattling noises.

The sounds are coming from the basement.

My body was frozen in fear, but I forced myself to make it move. Breathlessly, I tossed the quilt aside, and slipped out of bed. Tiptoeing to the bedroom door, I took a deep breath then I slowly unfastened the lock.

I opened the door a gap, peering out with one eye. *The hallway was dark and quiet—did I turn out the hall light last night, or did someone else do it?* I wondered, my throat constricting.

For a brief moment, I almost believed that I'd imagined the sound below.

But then I heard another clank and I leapt back from the door, clutching my chest in horror.

Despite my fear, there was something else growing inside of me … *anger. How dare someone make me feel afraid in my own home?*

Could it be those teenage girls again, playing more pranks to try and scare me?

Determined, I thrust the door open and stepped out into the hall. It was dark, but there was a beam of light shining from the stove top in the kitchen.

The hallway was empty.

I tiptoed down the hall and through the kitchen. The door to the basement was right there, in between the living room and kitchen. It was usually kept closed up tight, but now it was ajar.

Impulsively, I grabbed a bread knife from the counter and gripped it stiffly in my palm.

I opened the door and shouted, "Who's down there?" My voice not my own, thick with fear and something else … *adrenaline.*

With the knife held out in front of me like a shield, I took two nervous steps down into the dark hole.

"I've called the police! Who's down there?" I bellowed.

I nearly fell back on my haunches as a moon-white face emerged at the bottom of the stone staircase and stared up wearily at me.

"It's only me," Chrissy said. "Your pilot light went out. Heat's not working. I was trying to fix it for you."

There was a grill lighter in one of her hands and a screwdriver in the other.

Her eyes traveled from my face to my hand, widening as she saw the knife.

"What's that for?"

"Why didn't you wake me up? I heard something ... I thought..."

Chrissy frowned. "I tried. Your door was locked."

She tried to open the door to my room?

I lowered the knife, but kept it tucked close to my side. Nervously, I climbed down the stairs to meet her.

One dusty yellow bulb was lit, illuminating my washer and dryer, and the furnace.

And the plastic tubs of family photos and documents. Immediately, I noticed that the lids were gone from two of them—*did I do that when I came down here months ago, or was she snooping through my stuff?*

"I'm sorry if I scared you," Chrissy said.

"I wasn't scared." I moved past her to get a better look at the tubs. The lids were lying on the floor a couple of feet away. *She was definitely snooping.*

"No offense, but you're holding a knife. I think I scared you, and I'm truly sorry. Can you set that down, please?"

She was so close to me; I could still smell last night's whiskey on her breath. Her hair was disheveled. Her clothes the same, wrinkled outfit from the night before.

"You know how to fix a furnace?" I asked, finally resting the knife on top of the dryer.

"Somewhat. But I think it's just the pilot light. I had to light ours all the time in the trailer when I was a kid."

I tried to imagine Chrissy, a young child, fiddling with the gas on her furnace. It made me sad. She hadn't lived an easy life, not as a kid or an adult.

In the cavernous cellar, yellow light cast strange reflections off her new hair color. Combined with the sickly glow of the room, the color resembled that of a bruised apple.

I took a seat on the bottom stair, probably coating my sweatpants in mold and dust, but I didn't care. I felt tired and wiry.

As I watched Chrissy kneel on the floor in front of the furnace, I shivered. It was so cold down here, my breath forming icy puffs in the air.

"Are you sure you know what you're doing?" My teeth chattered uncontrollably.

"I think..." she muttered, turning a switch and lifting the lighter to ignite the pilot light. "There we go. It's lit now. Hopefully it stays on this time." She remained there for another minute, holding the button and examining the tiny orange flame inside it. Then she replaced the panel, as though she'd done it a million times before.

My mind fluttered back to Jenny's hands ... those eerie burn marks ... everyone had assumed they were torture marks, inflicted by the killer—but could she have burned them on something earlier in the night?

"You okay?" Chrissy asked, getting back on her feet, knees cracking.

"Yeah, I think so. Thanks for fixing that. It's been fucking up for weeks now..." I placed my head in my hands, elbows resting on my knees as I sat on the dirty old cellar step.

"Again, I'm sorry if I frightened you..." Chrissy placed the lighter on a thin wooden shelf along with the screwdriver she'd used. I recognized it—the shiny red handle covered in grooves and nicks. I hadn't seen it in so long ... my father's tools.

"It's not that. I barely slept. I can't stop thinking about our talk, the things you said..."

"I was wasted, Natalie. I'm truly sorry. I have some extra money still. I'll use it to get a hotel tomorrow," Chrissy said.

"Drunk or not, I know you remember. You said there was someone else in that field. That you were covering for them ... I need to know who it was, Chrissy."

Chrissy shook her head, walking towards me as though she meant to skirt around me on the stairs and dart back up. I stood, blocking her way.

"I can't tell the story if you won't let me. You can trust

me, Chrissy. I will listen to anything you tell me. I'm willing to keep an open mind."

Chrissy gave me a steely look, her face hard like a mask. "You sure about that?"

"I am."

Her shoulders relaxed and suddenly, she seemed smaller and shrunken, inches shorter than before. "Then I guess you better sit down for this."

Chapter Nineteen

The chessboard was still a mess, my king defeated, slumped on his side from earlier.

"Just a minute." As Chrissy walked over to the thermostat, I stood my king upright.

He looks much better this way.

She tapped the dial, then perked her head up. A blast of heat whistled through the vents.

"It's working," she said, smiling weakly.

"Thank goodness. I'm freezing," I moaned.

Chrissy sat on the couch beside me. "You were suspicious when you saw me down there. You thought I was looking around."

"It's not that ... it's just..."

"Well, you're right," Chrissy finished. Her eyes were pupil-less in the dark.

I stared at her, dumbfounded.

"Why?" I asked.

"It needed re-lighting. Your pilot light, I mean … but that's not the only reason I went down there. I couldn't find what I was looking for upstairs."

I scanned her face for answers, a trickle of anger forming in the pit of my belly. *What's she playing at?*

"And what might that be?"

"Proof," Chrissy said, simply. She unfolded herself on the sofa beside me, resting her chin in her hands.

I leaned forward, smacking my palms down on the table with the chess board, surprising myself, as pieces scattered, knocked to the carpet below. "If you've got something to say, go on and say it. As much as I want to help you, I'm sick of you talking in circles."

But instead of talking, Chrissy leaned forward, her face mere inches from mine, and then she reached back for something in her back jeans pocket. She removed it and placed it in the center of her lap.

A single piece of lined notebook paper folded into a square.

I plucked it up, narrowing my eyes at her as I unfolded this piece of so-called "proof".

I scanned the words, unblinking, then tossed it back at Chrissy.

"It's a note that Jack wrote, telling my mom he's going out with friends and he'll be back by curfew. It's not dated. And if you'd taken the time to look around more down there, then you'd have found hundreds of ones just like it.

My mom was a pack rat. She saved everything. Notes and papers and stupid drawings. I wouldn't be shocked if my baby teeth and hair are tossed in one of those tubs downstairs ... why is this important?"

Chrissy frowned. "His name isn't on it. How do you know your brother wrote that?" she asked, tapping her finger patiently at the top.

Why is she obsessed with a scratchy old letter Jack wrote as a kid decades ago?!

"I know it's his writing..." I stared at Jack's words, my voice suddenly thick with grief. "I know because I've seen his writing a million times ... when he, when he was still alive."

I stared at the letters, my eyes burning and threatening to tear up ... the loopy Ps and the blocky Bs...

"But you didn't recognize it when you read his letter in my box, did you?"

I narrowed my eyes at the letter, head tilting to the side as I tried to remember the words. *Come on. Sneak out and meet me tonight. Let's have our own party, beautiful. -J*

My breath lodged in my throat. I shook my head, looking up at her and back at the letter.

"You and my brother ... but I thought those letters were from John?"

I don't believe her. If she and Jack were together, I would have known. Right?

"Wait here," I said, stiffly.

Moments later, I returned to the living room with her

shoe box of crap in my hand. I'd barely glanced at it the other night, planning to come back to it, but I still hadn't...

I took the letters out, one by one, setting aside the one from Jenny and John.

As I held the mysterious J's letter next to the one of my brother's, there was no denying it now. *How come I didn't realize before?*

"In your defense, you probably haven't seen your brother's handwriting in years." Chrissy's voice was soft, like a thousand tiny whispers in the room.

What does this mean? Why is she telling me this now?

"He would have told me," I said.

Chrissy smiled, but there was something empty behind it. Something sad.

But would *he have told me? If he was having a relationship with our neighbor across the creek, we would have known about it, surely...*

My thoughts swirled with memories of Jack at that age ... around the time of Jenny's death, he was so private, fiercely protecting his space, his inner world... We were close, but as a teen ... he pulled away from me then. Nothing was the same after that summer Jenny died. Nothing was ever right again with my family.

"Your brother was a good man, and I was devastated when I learned of his suicide," Chrissy said.

"You said you didn't know," I growled. *First, she pretends she didn't know he was dead, and now she acts like she mourned for him? Implies there was something going on with my brother that I didn't know about?!*

I could feel my fingers balling into tiny fists, rage versus confusion in my head.

"He had these stupid binoculars ... always watching me from his window. I loved to sneak through the trees at night, crossing the river, and I'd stand at the edge of the tree line and wave ... sometimes he'd sneak out and meet me there. He was gentle ... and kind. The only boy in this town who truly seemed to like me for me." Chrissy's eyes were watery, lost in thought.

For some reason, the mention of his prized binoculars broke something inside me. I gasped with grief, tears flooding down my face now...

Chrissy reached a hand across the table, touching mine. I jerked back, surprising myself and her.

"So, my brother had a crush on you? That doesn't mean he hurt Jenny. He wasn't even here on the night she died... He was staying with my Aunt Lane then. Because that's what you're implying, isn't it? I'm not stupid, Chrissy."

Chrissy frowned. "I know that's what they told you, but I saw him the night before ... he was here, in the house and the next day..."

"No." I shook my head back and forth like a whiny toddler.

"For the longest time ... I thought ... I thought maybe he ... he..." Chrissy sputtered.

"No. Don't even say it," I warned.

163

But Chrissy wouldn't stop talking. "When I saw her that day, crossing the field ... I thought she was coming to me. But she wasn't. She was on her way to your house."

I leaned forward, elbows grinding into the edge of the forgotten chess board.

"Don't you see? She wanted to deal with the John situation the way most girls do ... she wanted revenge. Jack liked her, of course he did! Every fucking guy in this town swooned over Jenny! And my first thought was: she's going to get back at me by sleeping with the guy I love. I slept with John and now she's going to take my Jack..."

Hearing Chrissy refer to my brother as "her" Jack made my stomach coil in disgust.

He wasn't *her* Jack. He was *mine* ... *my brother*, who I thought told me everything. Who I loved more than life itself... My mind flashed back to his lifeless body on the bedroom floor, his skull blown to pieces with our daddy's gun. Did his suicide have anything to do with this? *Nonono...*

Oh, Jack. What kind of secrets were you hiding from me, from us...?

Chrissy said, "The next time I saw Jenny, she was lying dead in the field. The sun hadn't come up yet. And I wasn't wearing shoes out there ... I rarely did. So, I don't know how those muddy Converse got in my closet. They were mine, but I didn't put them there ... and Jenny was with your brother before she died. That's all I know..."

Chapter Twenty

Three truths.
One lie.
Chrissy Cornwall loved my brother.
My brother loved her back.
Jenny tried to hook up with him to get revenge.
Chrissy didn't kill her.

I threw my wallet on the kitchen table, then started digging. I fished out two twenties and a couple ones and thrust them into Chrissy's hand.

"Here's money for a cab or Uber. I'll even call one for you. But you have to leave. I need time to think."

When she made no move to leave, the money frozen in her hand, I said, "Please."

Chrissy looked like she was on the verge of tears. As bad as I felt for tossing her out, I couldn't deal with her being here for one second longer. *If she's implying that my brother killed Jenny ... no. No, I refuse to believe that.*

"I can't think straight. My head is throbbing..."

"But you didn't even let me finish. I don't necessarily think your brother killed her. I don't have proof of that..." Chrissy said.

I was shaking, my head spinning like a tilt-o-whirl.

"Those first several years in prison, when he never wrote me back or came to see me ... I was devastated. But then, he did. He was like an angel on the other side of the glass, with that messy hair of his ... he hadn't changed a bit..."

My brother visited Chrissy in prison? This is news to me...

"I thought he'd come to tell me the truth. To thank me for taking the fall. But then he asked me why I did it. Said he'd been trying to forgive me those first couple years but couldn't understand. When I told him about Jenny going to the farmhouse, that I saw her going to see him ... he swore he never slept with her. He said they talked for a while, then she went home. He thought all along that I was the one who killed her as she left that day. And I thought it was him who did it ... I thought I was covering for him. Proving my love."

"Well, of course he thought you did it, Chrissy, you confessed!" I said, exasperated.

"But I did it to protect him, don't you see?! He never

told the cops he was with her the night before. And … and … I thought I was doing the right thing. His future was so much brighter than mine…"

"That's such bullshit, Chrissy. My brother didn't kill her. He wouldn't…"

But Chrissy was rambling now, talking more to herself than to me. "I— I thought he and I were the only ones who knew the truth. But, as it turns out, neither of us really knew it. I swore to him it wasn't me … but, just like you, I don't think he believed me. He said he saw her that night. He admitted to me that he was hanging out with her, even kissing her … but he swore she left. So, somewhere between your house and mine, that little girl was murdered. I thought it was him. He thought it was me. If it wasn't one of us, who was it? That's what I'm trying to understand. That's what I need you to see…" Chrissy whined.

I allowed myself to fall back in one of the kitchen chairs, my head and heart pounding with disbelief. *How could any of this be true?*

Sure, there were all sorts of wild theories online. The conspiracy theorists on Reddit loved to pick apart the case. I'd read theories about my mom and dad … and Chrissy's brothers and parents. Hell, some of the theories even cast blame on Jenny's own parents and the local police chief. But they were all just tales … never any evidence to support them. And Jack was cleared right off the bat, because he was staying with my Aunt Lane. *Supposedly…*

Chrissy turned away slowly, and I watched as she

trudged upstairs. I sat at the kitchen table, wondering if she would stay after all. I shouldn't force her to leave … she seems honest, like she's telling the truth … *but this isn't the truth I want to hear.*

Moments later, I heard the jingle of her backpack. Slowly, she came back down the stairs, barely glancing back at me as she turned to go.

At the doorway, she froze momentarily, shoulders slumped in defeat. This was a much different version than the Chrissy who preached on my porch that first morning like a messiah. She looked defeated.

I considered stopping her. Telling her to just stay … to just give me a minute to process, to think … But then I heard the soft thud of the front door closing.

The taxi money was still on the table.

Chapter Twenty-One

Although my head was spinning, my stomach twisted in knots, I collapsed into my parents' old bed, tucking the blankets up to my chin. Within seconds, I was sleeping, dreams wild and fitful. Memories unhinged.

As I cracked my eyes open hours later, it all came rushing back. *Jack might have been involved in Jenny's death. There's something I'm missing here ... something we've missed all along. As much as I don't want to believe her, I do. I do believe Chrissy...*

Throwing the covers off, I was shocked when I saw the clock. It was after two in the afternoon.

For a brief moment, I couldn't even remember what day it was. But then the rest of it came flooding back—Chrissy and the letter from Jack...

If what she said was true, then Jack was the last person to see

Jenny alive. Did Chrissy do it or did he? Or was there someone else out there that day … John Bishop, perhaps?

In the kitchen, I flipped on the coffee pot and leaned against the counter, staring at the room as though I'd never seen it before.

The shoe box was still on the table. Beside it was Jack's hand-written letter Chrissy had scrounged up from the cellar.

It was the same bright red Formica table we'd had since I was a child, one of the few remaining pieces from a life long gone. *Gone but not completely forgotten.*

If I closed my eyes, I could almost see us there—Jack at the end of the table, gangly arms reaching, always reaching, for more food. Mom smiling at the other end, although usually she was on her feet, passing food or refilling cups of milk … reheating my father's broccoli and meat.

And Dad. He was always quiet and stern at the table, food sectioned off into perfect little portions, never touching. He ate slowly, methodically, and he laughed when we teased him about it.

Me. *Old-me.* Hair always in braids or a high ponytail, I sat on the opposite side, facing Dad. Close enough to kick my brother under the table, or fling potatoes at him when Mom wasn't looking.

For so many years, I'd replayed that morning … peeking through my brother's window, that awful dead girl in the field…

She Lied She Died

I knew that Jack was gone, visiting with Aunt Lane. *But how had I known that?*

I'd focused for so long on that one moment, that one day … but what about the night before? Closing my eyes, I tried to rewind the tape … tried to replay the events from before.

I had been with Adrianna until late that night. *But why was I with her?*

And then it dawned on me: Girl Scouts.

Often times, Adrianna's mom picked us up from our Girl Scout meetings and dropped me off at home afterwards. Mom was working part-time at the grocery back then, because the farm was losing steam. They tried to hide their money problems from us, but Jack and I always knew. And we heard them fighting, angry words shout-whispered in the dark.

In truth, the only part about her leaving that truly hurt was the fact that she left *me* when she did. I was fourteen at the time—at an age where I didn't think I needed anyone, but in truth, I needed my mom more than ever. We grew apart after that, Jack and I, and things with Dad too … I just wanted to get far far away, leave this shithole like Mom did.

But on that particular night, the night before we found Jenny … I squeezed my eyes, straining, willing my brain to cooperate. To *remember*.

Mom picked me up from Adrianna's house. It was late. I know it was late because I was falling asleep on the way home.

Was Jack home when I got back?

171

That I couldn't remember. As far as I knew, I'd gone straight to bed when I got in.

It was the next morning that I heard the sirens ... that I woke up to the terrible sight. The terrible news about a girl I barely knew, Jenny ... and Jack wasn't there. I didn't see him until days later when he got back from visiting our aunt.

If Dad was gone that night, which he might have been, and Mom was working late ... and I was at my Girl Scout meeting and then at my best friend's house, then it was possible that Jack was alone in the house. That he could have brought Jenny inside. That he could have done it...

No. My brother wouldn't kill a person.

He had no *reason* to kill her.

He barely knew Jenny Juliott ... but then, I thought about Chrissy, referring to the times she saw Jack at those parties. *How did I not know he was hanging around with that crowd? What else did I miss?*

My mind flashed back to my brother, lifeless and bleeding on the bedroom floor ... *there were many things I'd missed, apparently.* I didn't want to believe there was a specific reason he ended his life, but maybe ... *maybe he felt guilty all along.*

I filled my coffee cup to the brim and carried it carefully to the front porch, blowing steam from the top. The autumn air was cool and crisp, chunky gray clouds forming in the east, hovering low beyond the trees.

I took one long, burning sip of my coffee and left it behind on the top porch step.

Hands tucked in my pockets, I crossed the field.

The ground was cold and hard, my tennis shoes squeaky and thin as I made my way through the desolate farmland.

Once upon a time, this farm was thriving. Dad had some cattle. A couple goats and chickens.

He grew oats and corn. Some potatoes and vegetables. Not a lot, but enough. Mom helped too.

It was less of a money-making endeavor, and more of a family tradition. My father's father had been a farmer in Nebraska. And my mother came from a long line of farmers too. They were perfect for each other, in the beginning.

We like to grow things. Be self-sufficient. Take care of our own, Mom once told me.

On Sundays, she would sell fresh eggs at the farmers' market, but she barely made enough to cover her stall fees. And as my dad grew older and my brother and I were less interested in helping, everything fell by the wayside … first, he sold the cattle to a larger farm in Illinois. Then the barn grew into disrepair, and when the chickens and goats died, Dad didn't replace them.

Even the crops eventually withered away, dwindling to dust…

And when my mother left … Dad gave up on the place completely. He maintained the grass, but that was it. Each morning, he slipped on his dumpy orange hat and thick jean coveralls, and he went to work at the cement plant.

With Mom gone, he stayed away more and more, as though, at times, he could barely stand the sight of us.

I opened the door of the rickety old barn, a flap of birds sending a tiny electric shock through me, leaving me breathless.

The barn was empty, besides a rack of old, rusty farm tools, stacks of crates for hay, and the ghosts of what might have been.

I hadn't expected to find Chrissy in here … but I wondered: *where did she go when she left last night?* She hadn't taken the money. The two twenties and ones left behind.

The closest hotel wasn't for miles. I wondered, stiffly, if she went back home to Dennis.

Although the barn looked worn and abandoned, there was gravel covering the old dirt floor. It was growing thin beneath my feet.

It embarrassed me that I wasn't taking care of the place like I should be. Jack hadn't made a lot of changes when he'd lived here by himself, but he had added some things … the carpet (that he later destroyed with his own blood) and the gravel outside in the barn. He'd also repainted cabinets and walls … I'd done nothing of the sort since taking over, besides moving out his old stuff and repairing the damage to his room.

Why am I even still here?

As I closed the heavy wood door of the barn behind me,

I realized my hands were numb, the soles of my feet pure ice through my thin, insufficient sneakers.

But instead of heading back to the farmhouse, I marched for the trees.

As I crossed the tree line, entering the thin patch of trees between our property and Chrissy's, I turned to get a good look at my view from here.

There, wide and clear … my brother's window. With binoculars, he would have had a good view of Chrissy if she were standing here.

I tried to imagine Chrissy, young and beautiful, beckoning my brother to the woods … Mom and Dad wouldn't have liked it. The Cornwalls and the Breyases didn't talk much, even though they were our closest neighbors.

It had been years since I'd gone through these woods. When I was very little, Mom and Dad let me run and play on the farm and explore the woods with my brother. They warned me to be careful in the creek, but for the most part, they let us run free.

Until Jenny died.

After that, the whole landscape changed—the farm falling into disrepair, my parents keeping a tighter leash on Jack and me. We spent very little time out here after that—our lives mostly changing, as it so often does for teens; our interests centered on our friends and our privacy, tucked away behind closed bedroom doors. Locked up inside trunks.

Hidden in the secrecy of letters…

And for some, like Mom, it was easier to leave it all behind.

Maybe she had the right idea.

The path was overgrown, barely visible now, but my feet knew the way, and as I trudged through the woods, brushing branches and thickets from my hair and arms, I could hear the soft babbling sounds of the creek.

I had expected it to be dried up after all these years. But it was full from the recent rainfall, a strip of muddy current running rapidly downstream.

Trickles of rain pinged down from overhead, colliding with the leaves and the branches of the forest, creating a chilly mist that coated my hair and face.

In the foggy reflection of the stream, I stared at my shapeless face as it waxed and waned, trying to imagine Chrissy, or my brother, spending time down here as kids. *How did I not know he was sneaking out?*

The creek was fairly shallow, if I remembered correctly, barely to my knees. But it was freezing and there was no way I wanted to wade across it this time of year.

I looked leerily at my destination on the other side.

I could have used the old farm road to reach the entrance of the Cornwalls' old property, but for some reason this felt right—following the path my brother and Chrissy would have taken during their nighttime rendezvous.

This part of the creek was too wide; I moved east, following the flow of water, until I reached an old overturned tree, bridging a gap between the twenty feet it took to get across.

Even at its narrowest point, my legs were too soft and slow to jump ten feet to the other side.

The log was my best bet now. I stuck out my right foot, tentatively, testing its strength. It was twisted and rotting in places, but it felt solid enough to hold me.

I took a deep breath and stepped on, swinging my left foot around in front of the right. I took three baby steps, then wobbled, raising my hands straight out on either side for balance.

The wood felt decidedly unsteady now, but after several more steps, it was too late to turn back.

In my youth, I probably could have run across it, prancing like a prized gazelle to the other side, no problem...

But now my gait was wobbly and slow, and I felt less sure than before.

I took one more step, then suddenly, my right foot slipped out from under me. I plunged forward, arms flailing desperately ... then my chest smacked the log with a painful thud.

"Ugh." I laid there, belly down on the log, for what felt like several minutes. The fall had knocked the wind out of me, and I struggled to suck in a deep breath of air.

I need to go to the gym, or something. I'm way out of shape these days...

I considered trying to stand back up, using my hands

and feet like a primate to get across. But that felt stupid, like some sort of backward evolution, so instead, I scooted across the rest of the way, tearing up my hands and the butt of my pants the whole way to the other side.

I was almost, blissfully, to the very end of it when I could have sworn I heard a tiny whistle of laughter.

"Who's there?" I squeaked, looking left and right through the trees. I stood up, once again using my arms for balance, and I leapt the final foot to the shore, feet slamming so hard on the ground that my teeth rattled.

This time the laughter was loud and clear, a wild chuckle ricocheting through the trees.

"Hello? Chrissy…?"

A blur of wild black hair swished by in the distance, and then there was someone else there too … a boy. They were running, a young girl and boy, heading straight for the Cornwalls' old property.

I imagined they were Chrissy and Jack. Secret lovers racing amongst the trees…

But as I followed their path, emerging on the other side, I saw two young teenagers who in no way resembled my brother or Chrissy.

However, I did recognize one of them—that girl again, the one from the other day … Amanda Butler, Adrianna's daughter.

"You again. Why are you here? This is trespassing, you know." I glared at them both, huffing, trying to catch my breath, as I stepped out into the Cornwalls' old yard.

Amanda frowned at me, lifting a lit cigarette to her mouth. She blew out a ring of smoke then said, "This isn't your property, lady. This here used to belong to the Cornwalls."

The boy beside her was tall and gangly; he looked two or three years older than her. He had an earing and a strange haircut—long on top but shaved on both sides.

"Yeah, so leave us alone," he said tactlessly, rolling his eyes at me.

"The Cornwalls don't live here anymore. That trailer there is abandoned. Probably not even safe," I said.

Amanda exploded with laughter and her pseudo-edgy comrade laughed too.

"This property belongs to the county now. And kids come here all the time. It's safe inside and I know that because I've been in it a million times," Amanda said, nastily.

"Yeah, it's a shit hole but nothing's wrong with it. We're just having a little fun, so get the hell out of here," the young man snapped.

"I'll do no such thing, young man," I said, painfully reminding myself of my old-lady status. "What are you doing out here anyway? Shouldn't you be in school?" I directed my question at Amanda.

Amanda rolled her eyes and took another drag, but I could tell that my comment about school concerned her.

"If you don't tell me, I'm going to call your mom. I bet she doesn't know you're out here."

I glanced past the kids, taking in my view of the trailer for the first time in years. It was dilapidated, the old white siding rotted, and green streaks of dirt and mildew licking up the sides of it. As my eyes traveled to the front, I spotted crude letters painted on the front door. Someone had graffitied the word TRASH in blocky black paint.

"Did you do that?" I asked, pointing.

"No! It's been that way for years," Amanda hissed, defiantly.

"Fuck this. Let's get out of here before Winslow spots my truck ... this bitch isn't worth our time, Amanda," the boy said, tugging at her sleeve impatiently.

I refused to look at him, studying the girl. She was trying to look and act older than she was, smoking a cigarette in her torn-up jeans and holey black T-shirt.

I knew her type. *Hell, I'd been her type at that age.*

Who knows? Maybe I still am.

She wasn't even wearing a jacket; I fought the urge to ask her if she was cold. *Gosh, I really am turning into my mother. Or how a mother should be,* I thought, drearily.

"Why aren't you at school?" I asked again.

Amanda pursed her lips together. "We got out early today. Teacher meetings, or some shit."

I highly doubted that were true, but I let it slide.

She looks so much like her mother at this age. That hair ... those eyes and nose ... the attitude.

"Your mom and I used to be friends; did you know that?" I blurted out.

Amanda stubbed the cigarette out, looking from the boy to me.

"Fine. Whatever," the boy said. I watched him turn his back on her, then skulk down the dirt road that led away from the front of the Cornwalls' old property. Moments later, his silhouette evaporated through the foggy mist that surrounded the trees. But I could still hear the heavy tromping of his boots on the ground.

"Yeah, I know," Amanda said, her response strangely delayed. "I know about you and my mom. She said you all used to be best friends."

Used to be. Until she turned her back on me when I needed her most.

"Your mom's parents—your grandma and grandpa, I guess—wouldn't let her come over to see me anymore. In the beginning, before Chrissy Cornwall confessed, the whole town treated my family like lepers. Like we were the ones who killed her. And even after the confession, the rumors continued for a couple years ... my own mom left town because of it. She couldn't take it anymore. Your mom and I were really close until her parents kept us apart..."

My cheeks flushed red, as I realized I was rambling to a girl who was less than half my age.

She gave me a bewildered look, then lit another cigarette.

"He your ride?" I asked, nodding in the direction her boyfriend went.

"Yeah, but I'm not worried. I'd bet a million bucks he's

still up there waiting for me. Probably spying on us through the trees!" she cupped her hands and shouted. As she turned back around to look at me, she had a big wolfish grin, teeth gleaming, and for a second, she was my best friend reincarnated.

"Why are you out here, Amanda? What are you guys looking for here? Setting up another prank for me, perhaps…"

When she didn't respond, I went on. "If it's a place to be alone together, I'm sure there's more romantic spots than this." I pointed at the ramshackle trailer.

Amanda snorted. "Pierre's not my boyfriend. We're barely even friends, really. We came here to look for the murder weapon. Rumor has it that she buried it here somewhere, or hid it inside the trailer…"

I scoffed at her. "Even if that were true, why do you care? Chrissy was already tried and convicted. She's served out her time…"

"Yeah, but I hear she's claiming she's innocent now. Is that true?" Amanda asked, wide-eyed.

Now it was my time to shrug.

"Well, it doesn't matter to me either way. But if we found it, can you imagine how much we could sell that fucker for on eBay? What if it's got her prints and shit on it, or someone else's … and it's been here the whole damn time?" Her eyes were bright with manic excitement.

I was shocked by her language and attitude but tried not to show it.

"Don't you think the cops would have found it by now? Or someone else?" I asked, hesitantly.

Amanda looked toward the ghoulish trailer but didn't respond. For the first time I noticed a green pack on the ground a few feet away from her.

"That yours?"

Amanda nodded. "I brought it with me. In case we find any evidence. Want to go inside? If Pierre's too scared to do it, then I'll do it myself. Unless … unless you're too scared too?"

I truly was a teenager again—getting teased and peer-pressured. *I don't miss those years, not even a bit.*

Every part of me said it was a bad idea. I had no right to be here, and what did I hope to find?

Plus, Adrianna would shit herself if she knew I was helping her daughter break into the county's private property…

"Sure. Let's do it," I said, decidedly.

Chapter Twenty-Two

As Amanda fought to open the front door of the trailer, I stared at the eerie black letters until they blurred before my eyes. TRASH. That's exactly what people thought of Chrissy back then. *And still, nothing has changed,* I thought drily. Guilt circled back ... *I shouldn't have told her to leave. I overreacted...*

"I don't get it," Amanda huffed. "Somebody told me that it stays unlocked. Kids have broken in so many times ... and I saw some broken windows in the back, but the last thing I want to do is explain to Mom and Dad why I need to get stitches..."

Amanda twisted the knob side to side, then kicked the front door with a childish grunt.

"I thought you'd been here a million times," I said, unable to hide my amusement.

"Yeah, well, I said what I said. Doesn't mean it was the truth."

Oh, how right she is. Just because someone tells us one thing, doesn't necessarily mean we should believe them.

Lies. People told them for so many reasons—to protect others, to protect themselves ... to protect their reputation. *How many had I told in my lifetime? And more importantly, how many had my brother told me?*

Over the last twenty-four hours, I was starting to suspect that I didn't know him at all.

"Watch out." I stepped up to the door. Amanda, reluctantly, took a step back.

The knob turned easily in my hand, but the door wouldn't budge.

"The frame probably expanded and contracted because of the cool weather," I breathed, knocking my hip against the side of the door, unsuccessfully.

I froze at the sound of heavy, quick-footed steps coming up fast behind us. As I turned around, I don't know what I expected—Officer Winslow running down the hill to arrest us, or Amanda's parents coming to beat me down ... or even Chrissy, her ghoulish face like a banshee shrieking in the low-setting fog ... but it was only the boy again. As he stepped onto the porch, the sunlight brushing his nose and acne-laden cheeks, I realized he was younger than I'd originally thought. Perhaps Amanda's age, after all.

"I got this," he huffed. Suddenly, he rammed his

shoulder into the door, immediately screeching with pain as the door gave way with his weight.

"Fuck me," he moaned, bent over in the entryway, clutching his right shoulder and bent at the knee.

Amanda and I looked at each other, an amused exchange between us.

"Who's the dummy now?" Amanda teased, stepping inside the pitch-black trailer. I followed her, closing the door a crack behind us, but hesitant to close it all the way.

"Hey, at least I got it open," Pierre moaned, looking satisfied but still out of breath.

Amanda glanced back at me again, rolling her eyes.

Low streams of light created thin, dusty prisms around the abandoned front room of the trailer.

This was, undoubtedly, meant to be the Cornwalls' living room at one time. In the light of day, there was nothing frightening about it. Just an empty living space, like any normal family would have.

But there was no furniture left behind, only a scattering of trash in the corner—probably from teenagers who had snuck in previously—and knotted old carpet painted with a thick layer of grime. And the smell ... it reminded me of an old hamster cage; the acrid smell of urine and waste causing my eyes to water.

"Let's go explore," Pierre told Amanda, leaning his face into her neck, purring something inaudible in her ear. *Only friends, huh? Another lie, I presume.*

Pierre pulled her by the hand, and I watched them

disappear through a moldy kitchen then a cavernous hallway.

I'd been in enough trailers to know the general layout—a living room, kitchen, and bedrooms on either side of it. I followed a narrow hallway to my right, stopping to shine the torch light of my cell phone over the crude graffiti splashed all along the walls.

I KILLED THE BITCH. I stared at those loopy letters, painted deep dark red like congealed blood, then kept moving. I stopped when I reached a door on my left—a tiny bathroom. Out of habit, I groped for a switch in the dark before remembering, ridiculously, that the trailer had no electricity. Even with the sunlight, the place felt like a tomb.

I held my cell phone light out in front of me, praying my battery would last a little bit longer, and puckered up my face at the disgusting remnants of Chrissy's old bathroom. It smelled like wet towels and urine, and it became obvious that vandals had been using the commode. The sinks were rusty from nonuse; the grout in the tiles was once probably gray or white, but it was smudged a slimy black color now.

At the end of the hallway were two narrow doors, in what I could only presume used to be Chrissy and her brothers' rooms. The door on the left opened into a small bedroom, no furniture left behind.

There's nothing here to see, I realized.

The walls were painted goose gray, the dingy old carpet fraying and curling at the corners. The floor felt wet with mold beneath my sneakers.

I peeked my head in the last room before entering. It was certainly Chrissy's old room. Floral wallpaper was peeling in the corners but most of the walls were covered in crude drawings and words.

ROT IN HELL CHRISSY.

YOU SHOULD KILL YOURSELF CHRISSY.

FUCK THE CORNWALLS.

FUCK YOU CHRISSY.

Shivering, I listened to the metallic popping of rain as it struck the metal roof of the trailer. I hadn't expected another storm so soon, but somehow, standing here now, it seemed fitting that one should arrive.

There was one window in Chrissy's bedroom, high and tiny. The walls were narrow, and a sad, oppressive aura washed over me.

There was a closet with pocket doors on the far side of the room, but the doors had been yanked off track. I stuck my head in the closet, almost expecting to see her muddy shoes on the floor, as they had been all those years ago in the police photos. *She said she was barefoot in the field that day ... if that's true, then how did her muddy shoes end up here, the prints matching those beside the body...? Did my brother try to frame her? But, if so, then why would he go visit her years later in prison?*

The room had been wiped out, either by Chrissy's family when they ditched it, or by people breaking into the property.

Do you feel Jenny there? I imagined Katie's words the

other day.

I couldn't "feel" her here either. Whatever that meant.

According to the late Officer Winslow's reports, they never found evidence of blood or any sort of crime scene in the Cornwalls' trailer.

This is not where she died.

But it was the place where Chrissy laid her head at night ... *were thoughts of murder swirling through her mind? Or was she truly focused on my brother ... and did she really allow herself to go to prison to protect him?*

Back in the day, they weren't using DNA evidence as they were now. Technically, Chrissy could have cleaned up the blood, and no one would be the wiser...

I stared inside the closet, the only remnants of Chrissy's childhood a few wire hangers pushed to the back. As I looked at them, feeling foolish for following these teens inside, I caught a glimpse of something from the corner of my eye.

There in the back of the closet ... a child's handwriting on the wall. I moved the hangers and squatted down, holding up my torch to read the words.

But they weren't words, only tiny letters: C.C. + J.B. = 4evr

Chrissy Cornwall and John Bishop, forever.

Or...

Chrissy and Jack Breyas, I realized.

Moments later, I was passing through the living room and kitchen, following the opposite hallway in the dark. A large master bedroom lay at the end of the hallway. As I peered inside the room, I shrank back as I saw what Amanda and Pierre were doing.

They were still clothed, but her back was against the wall, legs wrapped tightly around his waist as he pressed his body to hers.

"I'm going," I said, weakly.

Amanda's eyes popped open and she smiled at me over Pierre's shoulder, baring all her teeth.

Chapter Twenty-Three

Great Aunt Lane lived 90 miles north of Austin, in a town that looked eerily similar to Austin itself.

After a while, it's like all small towns are the same—boring yet full of secrets.

As I navigated the narrow lanes of Muncie passing by churches and cemeteries that looked just like the ones back home, I tried to remember how long it had been since I'd seen her.

Lane had to be nearing ninety by now, one of the few members of the Breyas family to make it beyond the ripe old age of seventy. She was rabbit-toothed and cadaverous, with a rosy, wrinkled face covered in tattooed makeup. At least that's how I always remembered her.

My father had always been so quiet; it was mind-boggling when people met his aunt. She was gabby and blunt, and whipper-snap thin to his fleshy, broad frame. They were nothing alike, at all.

The last time I saw her was at Jack's funeral.

She and a few distant relatives on the Breyas side had been the only family members in attendance. *The rest of us are gone. Or hiding, as is the case with my mother,* I thought bitterly.

Lane's house on Stony Brook Boulevard looked smaller than I remembered. It was old, built in the '70s, but it had been well maintained over the years. The shutters were painted a shiny sky blue, the siding appeared recently pressure-washed. And someone was obviously doing her lawncare. The shrubs that lined the pathway to her front door were perfectly sculpted into neat, pointy diamond shapes.

There was something soothing about being here though —Lane was the only real connection I had to my family anymore, even if we weren't that close. I knocked on her door, waiting breathlessly.

I didn't expect her to be so fast, but the door popped right open, Lane's big smile and shiny bright teeth welcomed me.

"Sorry I didn't call. I was in the neighborhood," I lied.

"Oh, honey. Come in! Come in! You don't need an excuse to visit me, silly child," she cooed.

As she let me in, she squeezed both of my shoulders, looking me over. "You look dead dog tired," she concluded, sizing me up.

"I *am* tired, Lane," I admitted, drily.

The sunken family room brought back a thousand memories. I'd only been here a few times as a child, but the memories had left their mark. There were still three bear cubs in the corner of the room, their painted faces vicious and strange. The fireplace mantel still lined with tiny knick-knacks—a black and white glass yorkie, a petal pink rose made out of plastic masquerading as metal ... and I could remember her never allowing me to touch anything.

"This place hasn't changed a bit," I said, smiling half-heartedly.

"Right. It hasn't but I have. I guess that's how it goes, right?"

I wasn't sure what she meant exactly, but I nodded, letting her lead me into her large dining space. The long pine table I remembered had been replaced with a smaller glass round one.

"Take a seat. I'll fetch you something to drink. But mind your prints on the table. I just got it and I hate cleaning fingerprints off the glass."

As I waited for her to come back with my drink, I kept my hands tucked neatly under the table in my lap.

I was here for one reason and one reason only. To ask her about that time when Jack came to stay with her.

But now that I was here ... I couldn't help thinking about my mother too. Lane was the only one still in contact with her. Over the years, my mother had sent her postcards and she'd forwarded some of them on to us as teens. I can remember a few birthdays, getting envelopes stuffed with dollars. But then, those eventually stopped too.

Lane returned, carrying a white flowery cup of tea. She sat it on a coaster in front of me.

I lifted it to my lips shakily and blanched at the bitter taste of it.

"So, how are you, dear? It's been too long since I saw your face," she said, sitting down beside me. She rested her well-manicured, paper-thin hands on my arm. The touch surprised me, but mostly it felt strange because I enjoyed it … how good it was to be touched by a family member after so long. I'd forgotten what that felt like.

"You've aged quite a bit though, haven't you?" she asked, abruptly.

I pulled back from her and sighed. *No, she hasn't changed a bit despite what she says*, I decided.

"Yes, I have. But you look great, of course. How are you, Aunt Lane?"

She smiled, something in the way her eyebrows moved reminding me of my father.

"I'm all right. Same-o, same-o. And I'm happy to see you, but I'm a little surprised. You should have called first," she said. *So much for not needing to call.*

"Sorry about that. I need to ask you some questions about Jack," I said.

Lane's face fell. "That poor boy. I'd kill him myself if I could, for leaving us behind the way he did…"

I flinched at the harshness of her words.

"Yeah … well, I wanted to ask you about a time he came to stay with you for a few days. He was young at the time, almost sixteen. Jenny Juliott was murdered while Jack was at your house. Do you remember that?" I asked, carefully.

Lane frowned. "Well, of course I do. I'm old, not senile. And how could I forget? He was here with me when we heard the awful news about that girl."

"When did he come to stay exactly?"

"Well, it was the night before it happened. Your father brought him to me. He wanted to stay with his Aunt Lane for a few days. We were close, remember?"

I did remember.

It had always bothered me how much she favored him, pinching his cheeks and doting over him on Christmas. Inviting him over, but then not me. Mom used to say it was because Jack reminded her of Daddy, and I reminded her of Mom. They were as close as in-laws could be, I guess, but I suspected there was some tension, or disconnect, between my mom and Lane. Which is why I found it so odd that they had kept up communication over the years…

She doesn't want to talk to her husband or children, but she wants to talk to old aunt Lane … and now there's only one of us left and she still doesn't care. I'll never forgive Mom for leaving us, I decided, heavily.

"I do remember that. But I was wondering why he came the night before. Was something wrong? I feel like I was so young … I can't put all the pieces of that terrible time back together in my head," I said.

Lane pursed her lips. "I don't remember a particular reason. Although you don't need a reason to visit family. In fact, I really wish you came around more often, Natalie."

"How did he seem while he was here?" I asked, skirting around her scolding words.

"He seemed okay. I think he was as okay as any boy at that age could be. He was caught in that limbo, you know? Stuck between being a child and a man. I think he wanted to get away from the farm for a few days."

"What time did he come that night? I'm impressed by your memory, auntie."

"Oh, don't patronize me, dear! I know about that awful woman getting out of prison, and I saw what's happening in the news. She's not innocent. You'd be a fool to believe that! And, frankly, coming around here, asking me all these weird questions about your brother … what is this nonsense about? I might be daft, but I'm not dumb. I know there's a reason or you wouldn't be asking. I don't think you'd be here at all if you didn't need something," she said with a sniff.

And there it is. That look of disdain. I do remind her of my mother.

No one was ever good enough for her precious nephew —my father—and for many years, she had snubbed my mother and me. And with Jack, she always thought he was better than the rest of us too…

"I'm just trying to get the details straight for the book, Lane. I want to explain how it seemed, from my perspective, that day. And I want to make sure I have the facts straight. If Jack wasn't there, then I don't want to mess up and put that in the book." I *was* patronizing her now, but I needed to stay on her good side to get more information.

"Well, your brother wasn't there when that girl was killed. He was with me, staying the night. Your mother brought him late that night, but that's because she was working that new job of hers and she got off late. And she had to pick you up from somewhere too…"

"I thought you said it was my father who brought him," I said, quietly, unsure.

Lane narrowed her eyes. "Well, I can't remember every detail. That's right … it wasn't either or. It was both of them that brought him. And he stayed here for two days. We had a lovely time, playing pinochle and singing Dolly Parton songs, if you must know."

I sipped the bitter tea some more, trying to work out the details. *If my brother didn't go over there until late, before my mom picked me up … then he would have had time to do it.*

Chrissy's story could possibly be true.

"When's the last time you saw my mother?" I asked, staring into my tea.

Lane sighed. "It's been years, honey. The last I knew she was living in Chicago with a new boyfriend. Or maybe it was Atlanta, I don't know … she wasn't forthright with the details. And it's been years since she bothered writing."

"Does she have a new family now?" I asked, tentatively. I never asked, my own personal rule. *If she didn't care about my life, why should I care about hers?!* But, suddenly, I felt the urge to know everything … to face it all head-on.

For that first year after my mother left, I asked about her all the time.

But then my sadness over her absence eventually hardened, evolving into rage then fizzling into adult disappointment. And after she didn't come to my dad or brother's funerals, I decided she was dead to me too. *She's not my mother no more. I mourned her "death" years ago.*

"No, I don't think so. She has a new man, but no new kids, if that's what you mean," Lane said, stiffly.

"When was the last time she wrote?" I asked.

Lane shook her head, then sighed. "It's been so long, honey. I think the last time I got a card from her was in 2014. There was no return address. I don't think she wants us to know where she is. She's moved on with her life, Natalie. I don't think she ever wanted to be a Breyas in the first place."

But that wasn't true … I had memories of my mother, smiling and happy. Not just with us, but Dad too. Her shiny locket swinging back and forth as she ran from me to my brother, pushing us on the swings. We fought for her love at one time … who got to sit beside her, who got to sleep in her bed, who got to ride up front with her in the car … who got to brush her shiny hair, "silver like the moon," I called it. But then we moved on, just like she did. We let her go. And Dad had let her go too … *she gave us no other choice.*

"Thanks for the time and the tea," I said, softly.

"So, that's it then? No more to say?" Lane huffed.

"I'm sorry. I have an appointment later," I lied.

As she walked me to the door, I could tell she was pissed at me. But that was Lane's way … always upset with something I said or did. The only ones who got a free pass when it came to Lane were Dad and Jack. Now they were gone, and I was all she had left…

However, I had a feeling that I wouldn't be seeing her much, if at all, anymore.

Chapter Twenty-Four

All I wanted to do when I got back to Austin was take a hot shower and sleep. I'd been wrestling with my own thoughts the entire drive, the radio knob turned all the way down to silent. *What does it matter if I never know the truth? Will the world crumble if I don't? This incident with Chrissy has put my job in jeopardy, and my sanity too. With Jack gone, I'll never know for certain if there's any truth to it ... it's not like I can dig him up and ask him.*

As I turned down the old farm road, I sighed with relief. My eyes were watery from exhaustion, the heat blasting through the vents of my car threatening to lull me to sleep...

I groaned when I pulled in, staring at the shiny Gold Toyota. Parking next to it, I glanced wearily over at Adrianna. She was leaned back in the driver's chair, arms crossed tightly over her chest. *I wonder how long she's been waiting.*

As I gathered up my bag off the passenger's seat, she was already out of her car. I stepped out of the driver's side, meeting her nose to nose.

"My daughter got caught skipping school today. Would you believe that?" Adrianna wheezed.

"It's not like we never did it," I said, nonchalantly.

"True. But here's the thing: she said that she was exploring the old Cornwall trailer. And guess who helped her get in?" Adrianna's jaw jumped in her cheek. She was furious.

I took a deep breath, leaning against the hood of my car. It was still warm, keeping my bottom side toasty in the chilly autumn air.

"Look. I saw her out there again, only this time she wasn't with that little girl Cally. She was with a boy. Some thug named Pierre. They were already trying to break in when I found them. I didn't do any helping..."

Adrianna scoffed at me. "And you didn't think to call me? I mean, you see two teenagers skipping school, vandalizing property, and you don't stop to think you should call their parents?"

"Well, the thought crossed my mind. But we're not friends anymore, Adrianna. I didn't even know she was your daughter till the other day ... and that boy she was with, he seemed like a real asshole. I thought it was better for me to go inside with her than him. She was determined to look around," I said.

It wasn't quite the truth, but it also wasn't a lie. I had been concerned for the girl, but at the same time, I'd wanted to check out the old Cornwall trailer myself.

Adrianna's face softened. "I'm sorry ... it's just ... she's a wild one, that girl."

I couldn't help it; I chuckled. "They say it comes back around, don't they? We weren't all sunshine and rainbows ourselves."

Something in Adrianna's face changed ... a loosening up of that hard, tough-girl façade. She smiled, softly. "Well, we weren't all that bad either, were we? We turned out okay."

Did we? I wondered. *I guess only time will tell.*

"Want to come in for a minute?" I asked.

Adrianna stared up at the old farmhouse. *How long has it been since she stepped inside?* I wondered. *At least thirty years...*

"Nah. I'd better get going... It's almost eight..."

"Come on. Just for a minute. Let's chat," I urged her. The truth was, I wanted to sit down and talk to Adrianna about as much as I wanted to talk to my aunt Lane earlier. But I had ulterior motives now ... I wanted to ask her about her witness statement. The one that claimed Chrissy had forced Jenny into her truck that day...

"All right. Just a few minutes though," Adrianna relented.

We were *thick as thieves,* as my mother once called us. At one point in our lives, I knew everything about Adrianna Montgomery—her favorite color and her favorite band, what she wanted to be when she grew up … and she knew everything about me too. We were close, deep-in-the-bones close, and then Jenny happened.

After the murder, Adrianna's parents would no longer let her hang out with me. But they couldn't stop her from talking to me at school … *she made that choice all on her own.*

Staring across the table at my old best friend, I realized she was a stranger. I knew nothing about her life now. And all she knew of mine was what was in the news.

"How's your husband … what's his name?" I asked. I'd made coffee for us, but no matter how much I drank, I couldn't get the fragrant tea flavor from Lane's out of my mouth.

"Amanda's father's name is Chuck. But we're not together anymore," she said, briskly.

"Ah. Sorry to hear that."

"Well, I'm not sorry. The man is a turd. He comes in and out of her life. Frankly, I think that's one of her biggest problems. She's angry at him, so she takes it out on me," Adrianna explained.

I could understand that. As a child, it was easier to get upset with Mom than Dad. I expected more of her, so when I was upset about something, I wanted *her* to fix it. *I needed her to.* Then after she left … I turned all my anger inwards, forming a neat little cocoon around my heart.

"What about you? Never married?" Adrianna slurped her coffee.

I hated this question, but I'd heard it a hundred times. "No. Never married."

The truth was, I hadn't met anyone whom I could even remotely imagine spending the rest of my life with, or, worse, having children with. I'd dated a couple guys in college, but those were mostly fun flings that didn't last more than a couple months. I always thought there would be time for more … but now, I was back here, in the revolving door of Austin. And I didn't see any romantic prospects in my future here.

"And how's the interview with Chrissy going?" Adrianna frowned at me over her coffee mug.

"You know I can't talk about that. I'm still trying to put the pieces together," I said.

Adrianna quirked one eyebrow at me, just like Amanda had only hours earlier. The mother and daughter were more alike than they realized.

"Do you really believe she's innocent?" Adrianna asked.

I had half a mind to tell my old friend the truth: yes, I did. But, considering that she was a journalist, it didn't seem safe to discuss it yet.

"I'm not sure of anything," I said, which was pretty close to the truth. "I did come across something interesting though … I had no idea it was you that saw the girls in the parking lot that day."

I could have sworn Adrianna's face changed from tan to gray in that moment. "Who told you that?"

"I saw it in the police file." There was no reason to hide the fact that I'd seen it there; eventually, in the book, I would have to share most of the information anyway. "Why didn't you tell me, Adrianna?"

Adrianna sighed deeply, nudging her mug away. She was still wearing her wedding ring, I noticed. She spun it round and around on her finger, a nervous habit I'd forgotten she had. Although, back when we were kids, it was a best friends ring in its place. I was the one who gave it to her. *B.F.F. Best Friends Forever.* Another lie we told.

"My parents didn't want my name to get out there in the papers. As you know, the press wasn't kind back then … dragging everyone's name involved through the mud."

I couldn't help it: I smiled. "Oh, I do know. And I remember your family very explicitly turning their noses up at mine."

They were friends once—the Montgomerys and the Breyases—our parents playing cards and drinking beer on Friday nights, while Adrianna, Jack, and I played hide-n-seek upstairs. Having Adrianna as a friend was one of the sure things I had in my life, and I lost her and Mom just a few years apart…

"It wasn't my fault my family did that. All this time, you act like I chose to end our friendship. But I didn't. You were my best friend. It was my parents to blame, not me. I was hurting too."

I nodded. She was absolutely right. "I'm sorry. I never really thought of it that way," I said, meekly. "But you abandoned me at school too ... that hurt a lot."

"I'm sorry. I don't know why I did it ... I guess it hurt less to just let you go. My parents were so adamant about staying away from you and your family," she said.

"I'm sorry, too. You were a kid then. You couldn't help but be confused too. But ... I'm still surprised you didn't tell me about what you saw in the parking lot that day ... and that no one knew it was you who saw Jenny getting in the truck with Chrissy."

Adrianna's eyes looked wary in the dark kitchen as she thought back to that day. "Mom had me in that after-school babysitting program. So stupid. I didn't want to be treated like a baby anymore, but Mom didn't think I was old enough to be alone at home yet after school while she was still at work. Now that I'm a parent myself, I agree with her choice completely. The primary school got out earlier than the middle school, you remember?"

"Yes," I said. I'd stayed after school a couple times myself and I knew that the elementary school kids, especially those who were close to their primary graduation, liked to line up at the fence, looking out at the middle-schoolers as though they were demi-gods.

"You couldn't miss her. With that white-blonde hair and

those cool clothes … we all looked up to Jenny. She was gorgeous," Adrianna said, her voice so soft and sad.

"She was," I agreed.

"So, when I saw her talking to Chrissy Cornwall in the parking lot, I was shocked. Chrissy didn't even have her driver's license…"

"Did she really force Jenny into the truck?" I asked, tentatively.

Adrianna surprised me by shaking her head. "I never said that. The papers like to exaggerate. The cops too. As a journalist, I totally understand that now. But they *were* fighting … screaming, even … I didn't lie to the police about that. I only wish I could have known what they were saying exactly."

Chrissy claimed that she and Jenny were friends … that it was a planned ride-around after school. *So, why were they arguing then? Or could Adrianna be mistaken about what she saw…?*

"How did you know they were fighting?" I asked.

Adrianna frowned. "Well, Jenny looked mad. Her face was red, and she was shaking her head. Then I heard them screaming. But I couldn't quite make out the words…"

"If they were fighting, why do you think Jenny got in the truck?" I asked.

"I'm not sure. She walked away from Chrissy, then Chrissy ran up and grabbed her by the arm. She was pulling. But it was less like forcing her in the truck, and more like begging. Does this really matter though?" Adrianna asked, breathless.

"What do you mean?"

"We know she did it, Natalie! She confessed. Why are you playing into this psycho's hands? I'm afraid she'll hurt you. You shouldn't be alone with her…"

I could understand Adrianna's concern, and maybe she was right. Maybe I was being naïve for trusting Chrissy … but I couldn't help it. Somewhere in that short period of time we'd spent together, I'd caught a glimpse of the woman underneath—the one before the murder, before prison … the girl with the wild sense of humor and sad smile of youth.

Chapter Twenty-Five

I stopped writing and stared at the ceiling, the soft songs of rain dancing on the roof. I hadn't written much, only 2,000 words, but it was a start. *You have to start somewhere, honey.*

My dad and brother didn't get my love for writing, but Mom did. She used to encourage me to do it and asked if she could read my stories when I was done. She loved to read, and I always dreamed of the day when I could see her flipping pages on a book with my name on the cover. *Maybe I'll find out where she lives and mail her a copy when the book is done.* Sign it: *the daughter you abandoned.*

I'd searched for her earlier, as I often did when I was bored. I couldn't find her on Facebook, or on Twitter or Instagram either. I searched public court records ... anything to indicate where she was. *Who* she was now.

My guess was that she was remarried—no longer a

Breyas. According to Great Aunt Lane, she'd never wanted to be one in the first place.

And Dad. *I wish he were still alive, so I could ask him about Jack. Did he know more than I thought he did? Was he covering for his son?* I wondered. *Did Mom know more too? Is that why she took off?*

I willed myself to focus on the only thing that mattered right now—the story. I scanned the words ... my experience in the field that day. *Was it too bland? Too matter-of-fact?* I wondered.

Either way, 2,000 words seemed like a good start. *You have to start somewhere, honey.* Mom's words were back, haunting me as I drifted downstairs to the kitchen.

The wind had picked up outside; it whistled through the trees, rattling the windows in the kitchen and the chimes outside.

A storm is coming. Real and metaphorical.

Am I ready for it?

I heard the crunch of tires on gravel, and for a split second, I wondered if Adrianna was back. *Or Chrissy*, I silently hoped.

But it was Nash Winslow again.

I opened the door, forcing a smile, before he had a chance to knock.

This time, Chrissy wasn't here to hide, so I welcomed him inside. "It's nasty out there."

"Sure is." He ducked his head to fit through the arch in the hallway.

The police file was sitting on the kitchen table, next to the shoe box.

"I'm guessing this is what you came for," I waved over at the file.

"Yeah. Was it helpful?" he asked, taking off his hat and knocking water off of the brim. His hair was close-cropped, unlike his father's, but the same, familiar deep brown. His father was way too old for me back in the day, just a silly childish crush. But I couldn't help thinking the son was closer to my age now ... *I wonder if he's married,* I thought. My eyes traveled down to his hand—*no wedding ring,* I noted.

I cleared my throat. "The file was helpful. But here's the thing ... what if Chrissy *was* in the field that day? What if she saw the body, but she wasn't the one responsible for the murder?"

Nash's eyebrows, like two fuzzy caterpillars, curled up quizzically. "How do you mean?"

"What if someone else was there? Someone she was protecting?" I tapped the file on the table, making sure the papers were straight. He took it from my hands when I offered it, the rough pads of his fingers lingering over mine for a beat too long.

"I guess it could have been a possibility ... if she hadn't confessed. But, that's just it, she did confess. Chrissy had motive and means, and she certainly had opportunity. Worst of all, she admitted to it. And she's done her time ... so the only one who benefits from this change in her story now is her. She gets the attention she wants, from the press and from you. But it's bogus. All of it. I said the same thing to Katie Juliott."

I thought about Jenny's mother, kind but sick. "It was hard for me to make out anything useful after my talk with Katie. For a little while, she actually thought I was Jenny."

Nash didn't look surprised, only sad. "My folks were friends with the Juliotts. She was in denial for so long. Spent half that year sedated. My dad tried to tell her … tried to explain who did it and why. But she didn't believe that Chrissy would do that. She didn't think she had it in her for murder."

"Then who did she think did it, if not Chrissy?" I asked, curious.

Nash flipped his fingers through the pages of the file, thoughtful. "She didn't know. My father looked into everyone … your family. Hers. John Bishop. He was playing football at a camp in Seymour that night, his alibi air-tight. And we tracked down every grifter, everybody in town with a record … nothing else panned out."

"When you said your father looked into my family, did he ever suspect my brother?" I asked, trying to be nonchalant.

"I don't think so. Your brother was staying with a family member."

I nodded, solemnly. "He was. He left for my aunt's house the night before she was found … But the thing is—if you remove Chrissy's confession, all you have is circumstantial evidence. Don't you agree?" I asked.

Nash made a sound, something caught between a laugh and a groan. "But that's just it, Natalie. She *did* confess. There's no mystery here. Just a sad old woman … trying to redeem herself."

"I don't know, Nash. There's something not right about all this."

"Those muddy shoes and the matching print in the field were pretty damning too. You can't forget about those," Nash reminded me.

His words hit home. Even if Chrissy's alternative story made sense of the shoes, the most obvious conclusion still implicated her guilt…

Trying to change the past at this point was fruitless.

Am I willing to write a version of the story that I can't prove, one way or the other? No, I decided. *No, I'm not.*

But Chrissy's confession tucked in the back of the file … a child's messy writing … even her confession struck me as odd.

I killed Jenny because I was jealous of her and John. I stabbed her with a kitchen knife and burned her. I threw the knife in the creek.

It was too neat; too easy. It made no mention of the strangulation or how the burns on her hands and face were inflicted.

And that knife was never recovered.

Thinking about that confession, it almost read as someone who felt forced to write it. Like she was hiding something, another piece of the story…and she was trying to be as vague as possible to implicate herself and get it over with it.

That would make sense if she was protecting someone else.

I stood up from the table, feeling restless. I wanted him to leave; wanted to climb in bed and sleep until my head stopped spinning with the lies, trying to make them truth…

"You're right. She confessed, ultimately sealing her fate. Thanks again for lending me the file," I said.

"Any time."

As I saw him out, he tipped his hat at me like an old-fashioned gentleman. He was handsome, even more so than his late father. If I weren't so caught up in this mess with Chrissy, so distracted by my own thoughts, perhaps I would have worked up the nerve to ask him out some time…

He was just about to get in the cruiser when he remembered something and stopped. For a brief second, I almost hoped he might ask me out.

"Uh … I don't think you're going to have to worry about Chrissy much longer. She's leaving town. I saw her a couple hours ago. Folks are pissed because she's staying at Rooster's, so I made a quick stop over there today."

So, that's where she went.

Rooster's was the shittiest hole-in-the-wall motel in three counties. It was rent-by-the-day or by-the-week. And if the guests there were disturbed by her, that was pretty sad because it was mostly frequented by dealers and prostitutes.

"She said she's leaving in the morning. Bought a ticket for a Greyhound bus. I think she said it was headed to Wyoming. Or maybe it was West Virginia..."

Chapter Twenty-Six

W hen I hear the word "seedy", I think about Rooster's.

I'd never stayed or hung around there, not in all the years I'd lived in Austin. It was mostly drifters and people passing through who didn't know any better. And then the dealers and hookers of course.

It was a long, one-story building, each tiny room connected to the next. The roof was caving in, the old red brick chipped and fading. *A sad little place*, I thought.

But for such a sad place, it was popping on a Friday night. As I pulled in, there were people standing in the old dirt lot, people sprawled on lawn chairs and huddled around in groups, talking excitedly.

As I parked and got out, the energy in the air was palpable. *Something is wrong.*

"What is it?" I asked a heavyset woman in a bright red

sweatshirt. She was smoking and watching, standing apart from the crowd of people.

Like a beehive, they were buzzing with excitement. But I saw no signs of Chrissy.

"That woman who killed that little girl's in there…" She pointed toward room 19. The door was ajar. I could see the flicker of a television; there was a strange staticky sound coming from inside.

That "woman" was a girl when she killed her and she might not even be guilty, I wanted to say. But I didn't dare correct the woman; I was just grateful she hadn't recognized me yet from the news.

"Are you talking about Chrissy Cornwall?" I asked her.

"Yup. That's her. Crazy, right?" She took a long drag from her cigarette.

And that's when I heard it … sirens in the distance. A sound that, even now, thirty years later, still gave me chills.

"Ambulance is coming! Let's hope they don't make it in time," someone chuckled from among the crowd. The woman beside me laughed.

"If I find out who called them, I'm whooping your ass!" another man in the crowd shouted.

"Why's there an ambulance? What's going on?" A trickle of fear ran through me. I looked at the woman and she looked back at me. She was smiling.

"Bitch tried to off herself, can you believe that? Took a bunch of pills, apparently. Somebody called for help, although I don't know why. Think they should just let her die in there ... slow and miserable and alone like that poor girl did..."

But I was no longer listening. I ran for the door, shoving my way through the crowd of angry gawkers. As I pushed my way through the motel door, I could see her.

Flat on her back in the bed, Chrissy was choking, an eerie rattle erupting from her mouth ... for a split second, her frantic eyes popped open and seemed to register mine.

Chapter Twenty-Seven

Don't *freeze. Don't freeze. This time you CANNOT FREEZE.*

I ran to her bedside, calling her name. She was convulsing and gurgling, which was terrifying ... *but at least she's breathing!*

Sirens blared in the distance ... *please hurry. Please hurry!*

I placed my fingers on her chin and tilted her head back, listening. Her breathing was very shallow, but still there, her eyes drifting shut on me.

This isn't like Jack. She's not gone yet. I can still save her...

"Stay with me, Chrissy!" I gave her a couple sturdy shakes, but when that didn't work, I tilted back her head again and gave two rescue breaths. Next, I moved to chest compressions, counting aloud as I went.

I could hear the buzz of people all around me, talking

and laughing. Like the death of this woman was some sort of celebration.

I hated them for it.

I hated Chrissy for doing this ... to me, to herself. Just like Jack did.

And I hated myself for sending her away ... for abandoning her when she needed me.

I continued the cycle: breathing, compressing, then listening for what felt like hours, my lips and arms growing heavy and numb...

When the paramedics arrived, I didn't even hear them coming. Someone had to shove me aside to get to her.

"Good job. She's still alive," one paramedic said.

I stood out of the way, the room spinning as I watched them take over. Moments later, I heard the most beautiful words, "Her pulse is thready, but it's there. I think she'll be okay. We need to transport her now though."

I watched them load her into the ambulance, barely breathing myself.

The people in the crowd were following ... chasing behind the ambulance, shouting obscenities or laughing.

I turned and looked at the room, really seeing it for the first time. *What did Chrissy take?*

There was nothing in the room to make it obvious, but I found her backpack under the bed. I snatched it up and looked inside.

An empty pill bottle of Oxycodone, the patient's name

blacked out with marker. *Probably bought from one of the dealers at the motel.*

It was easy to get drugs in these parts; easier than getting a job or affordable insurance, truly.

I clutched the empty vial in my hand, realizing that I needed to let the hospital know exactly what she'd overdosed on. As I tossed it back in the bag, between a tangle of clothes and toiletries, I spotted something else inside. A tiny piece of folded paper. A note written on one of the complimentary notepads the motel gave you.

The letter was addressed to me.

Chapter Twenty-Eight

Natalie,

Is it better to administer the truth in small doses, or inject it all at once? I used to think I knew the answer, but I know nothing anymore.

I tried to tell a pretty lie. I told Jenny that her boyfriend was pursuing me and that we had slept together. I thought that would be enough. Sadly, I thought if she believed he was a cheater that would deter her even more than the truth. We women are strange ... jealousy overrules fear most of the time.

Because I didn't "sleep" with John at that party. The sex wasn't consensual, do you understand? Her boyfriend was a rapey piece of shit. And when she got back with him, even after the cheating, I knew I had no choice but to share the ugly truth.

That's why we were fighting in the parking lot. She didn't want to hear what I had to say. She wasn't ready for the truth. But finally, I convinced her. I told her about the rape. I told her that I was going to the police the next morning. John Bishop was a rapist who had to pay. I couldn't let him do it to her, or some other poor, unsuspecting girl.

She was calm when I told her, understanding, but then she showed up over at Jack's (your house). For so many years, I thought she went there for revenge. I was right—but it was a different sort of justice she had in mind. She didn't want to steal the boy I loved; she wanted to destroy him. Just like she thought I was going to destroy John when I turned him in for what he did to me.

I think she accused your brother of rape. And maybe that's why he killed her … because I didn't, Natalie. I have nothing to lose, no reason to lie anymore. I did not hurt Jenny.

Jack never said he killed her, but I know he was hiding something. He said the proof was in the trunk. But I couldn't find any trunks when I stayed at your house and I was scared to tell you … maybe the trunk of his old car? I don't know and I don't think I even want to know anymore.

I'd rather leave this world, letting them think I did it. Let your brother rest in peace. He was a good man; I promise he was.

I want to be with Jack now. Do you think I'll see him where I'm going? Please pray that I do.

Love,

Chrissy

Chapter Twenty-Nine

As I drove home, my body shook—fear, cold, exhaustion, adrenaline ... I couldn't be certain which. *Why would Chrissy do this?* My thoughts jettisoned from guilty to angry to guilty again...

The proof is in the trunk.

Chrissy suggested a car trunk, but that wasn't it. My brother drove a truck before his suicide, and I'd sold it a few months after returning to the farm.

The windows of my car were all the way down, air pushing against me. The wind knocking me dangerously side to side on the road, like some unseeable force trying to stop me—trying to prevent the inevitable...

The proof is in the trunk.

Moments later, I was home, running through the drenching rains to get inside.

First, I dialed the hospital, breathily explaining the bottle

I'd found in Chrissy's bag. Not the letter. I told no one about the letter I found.

"Can I come to the hospital and see her? Is she going to make it?" I braced myself for the emergency room operator's answer. She sounded distant and busy, the squeaky sounds of a busy ER in the background.

"Only when, and if, she becomes stable, she can have visitors. But family only," she told me.

Family only.

But Chrissy had no family. And for the most part, neither did I.

"But will she be okay? Can you tell me that?"

The woman groaned on the other end. "I can't give out medical info, dear, okay? But … she's stable. Your friend is stable for now."

"Thank you," I breathed, hanging up the phone with a relieved whoosh.

Chrissy might have been ready to leave this town, this earth … but Austin and the powers of the universe weren't ready to let her go. *Not yet at least.*

Her suicide letter shook in my hand as I paced back and forth in the living room. I couldn't stop thinking about the Cornwalls' trailer, empty and desolate. No traces of the past left behind.

That wasn't the case with my family's farm. Evidence of our past was still here, *right here*, hiding in plain sight. Pictures and letters … boxes of stuff downstairs. But the real question was: *where is Jack's trunk?*

Because the moment I read the letter, I knew which trunk Chrissy meant. Not the trunk of a car, but his prized *trunk*—the place where he'd kept parts of himself hidden away as a boy.

Is that where he hid the murder weapon?

But I haven't seen that old trunk in years!

It had been years since I'd even thought about the trunk; it hadn't been here when I moved in, which didn't seem strange. Over the years, we'd all gotten rid of past toys and possessions ... not seeing it never struck me as odd, and frankly, I hadn't even realized it was gone.

I had no idea where to look for it. *Could there be another trunk he was referring to when he said that to Chrissy...?*

As much as Chrissy wanted to leave this world, with all of its "pretty lies" about murder, I had to know the ugly truth. If my brother did it, if he killed Jenny Juliott ... then I wanted to know.

I need to know what he was hiding.

I searched every closet upstairs first, although I'd been through all that before. There was very little, if nothing, left behind of them anymore. I'd stored it all in the basement.

For the next several hours, I sifted through box after box downstairs. Tub after dusty tub, cobwebs clinging to my face and hands...

There were letters and pictures ... family vacations and school pictures. A time when we were happy and normal, such a long time ago...

I searched for hidden alcoves or loose floorboards,

which seemed like something my brother would do. He loved adventure and mystery, always sending me on wild goose chases as a kid. Memories of him danced around my head, making me sick with grief. *His treasure maps—X marks the spot. His made-up plays and games. Catch the pirate and tie him to a tree. Avoid the lava in the grass. Find the treasure and save the girl.*

He always had the best hiding spots as a kid…

So many hours spent living in worlds that weren't real … *where did that brother go? The one that was fun and playful. The one who didn't keep secrets like this … I wondered.*

My thoughts circled back to the Cornwalls' property. It was conveniently close; an easy place to hide something. But the trailer was empty, abandoned … but, perhaps, it was worth taking another look…

The house shook with thunder, lights flickering in and out, as I moved from room to room. *What am I missing, Jack? Where could you have hidden such a large trunk?*

When I had moved in, there was no evidence of digging or freshly loose soil. But, then again, who knew how long it had been since he'd hidden his secret?… *If it's outside, I'll never find* it.

But, impulsively, I stepped out on the front porch, catching my breath. I was sweating, my thoughts spinning wildly out of control.

Will Chrissy live? Did my brother kill Jenny? And where is that fucking trunk?

I considered the possibility that my brother had the trunk stored somewhere else, like a storage unit.

But, by now, the rent on a unit would have expired. I would have known if he had something like that, right?

If I wanted to hide something heavy and large like a trunk, where would I put it?

Lightning cracked the sky, and, in the distance, the barn lit up like a ghostly black shadow in the flash.

I thought about the loft in the top of the barn. *The place where we hid so many times as children.*

Determined, I took off across the field, certain the barn was where I'd find the truth.

Chapter Thirty

As I climbed the old ladder to the hay loft, I was certain this was the place. It was large enough to hold a trunk, and several more items if Jack had wanted to store them here.

But as I stood at the top of the ladder, wobbling dangerously, I was disappointed to see nothing but old bits of hay and fodder for the animals that used to live on the farm.

My heart fell.

There's no path to the truth anymore.

Carefully, I descended the ladder, trying to fight off feelings of vertigo. Three steps down, I noticed something below on the floor of the barn. Bales of hay that looked perfectly normal, but there was something strange about them too. As I stared at them from the top of the ladder, I noticed something odd.

They were arranged in the pattern of an X.
My breath froze in my chest. *Oh, Jack…*
X marks the spot.

Chapter Thirty-One

T he storm had knocked out the power lines, the old house an eerie silhouette from across the field.

Lightning cracked the night sky, rumbling the walls of the barn as I dug, my only light the dim, flickering lantern on the ground beside me.

I was sweating, face covered in dust, and my arms that were once throbbing with pain were now completely numb with exhaustion. Baring my teeth, I flung another mound of dirt and gravel to the side and slammed the shovel back into the earth.

The barn had always had a dirt floor ... but it had been replaced with a layer of gravel before I moved in. *I don't know when Jack added the gravel, but it had to have been while I was away at college.*

I was terrible with measurements—always had been— and I had no idea how far I'd dug. *At least three, maybe four, feet?* I stood back, leaning dizzily on the shovel, staring at the worthless hole in the ground. *I'd kill for a glass of water right now.*

At this rate, it would take me a week to dig up the floors in this barn. There was no real reason to believe I was right —those bales of hay could have been arranged that way for any number of reasons ... *by accident, perhaps? Or, even if Jack arranged them that way purposefully, it doesn't mean there's something below them...*

My logic for choosing this spot now seemed stupid and faulty ... in fact, this whole theory that what lay hidden was somewhere here in the barn felt off.

But I've come this far. I might as well go farther.

Wiping sweat from my brow, I looked around the entire barn space, trying to guesstimate how much ground there was to cover.

If I dig much deeper, I'll reach the doors of Hell itself.

So be it, I thought, wearily.

The dusty lantern cast hazy shadows around the walls of the barn. I watched them dance, hypnotized by it, as pellets of rain drummed the roof of the barn like heavy artillery fire.

It's like a war out there ... no one I can trust, not my neighbors and certainly not my family. Living or dead: did I know any of them, really? How much can you truly know a person—like, *really* know them?

Groaning, I adjusted my grip on the shovel and smashed it into the dirt. I flung two, three, four more mounds aside

... and that's when I heard a thud. The metal shovel connecting with something...

I'd expected metal—the metallic clank of a knife, or weapon, evidence of Jack's crime buried below ... but as I scraped loose dirt from the surface, I recognized it immediately: the deep brown leather, the old-fashioned brass plates ... *here it is: my brother's trunk.*

I'd only dug enough to uncover the top third of it. Exhilarated that I'd found it, I grabbed the shovel and began, moving ten times faster than before.

A deafening blast of thunder shook so hard, I could feel it deep in my bones. But I didn't let it deter me ... I kept on, determined to get the trunk loose and see what was inside it.

I was shocked to discover I was crying—or was that sweat? No, it was tears, dirty black rows of them streaming down my cheeks.

I lifted the shovel and spent the next few minutes clearing the dirt completely.

Oh, Jack. What were you hiding?

Maybe there was a part of me—a small, unforgivable sliver—that already knew it was bad. *Once you find out, you can't un-know it.*

Pretty truths or ugly lies, which one do you choose?

With the dingy old trunk uncovered, I selected a hammer from my father's wall of tools. The rotted old padlock broke off with one steady tap.

I choose...truth. Always, truth.

I lifted the heavy lid, holding my breath.

At first, all I saw were cobwebs. A nest of them, thin and wiry. *Silver like the moon.*

But under that wiry wisp of gray, the rotting hair was attached to a rotting scalp ... and the shrunken dead face of my mother stared up at me.

Chapter Thirty-Two

Rotting bits of blue fabric clung to her chest. Her skeletal legs were bent—she'd obviously been folded and placed inside it.

The fabric on her body had decayed, but I could still pick out the pattern … one I'd seen a thousand times. My brother's old *Star Wars* blanket. The very same blanket I puked on the morning I saw Jenny's bloated body, rotting in the sun, through my brother's binoculars.

My mother's hair was all that was left, the flesh on her face rotted away, but those teeth … that face … and the heart shaped locket at her neck … there was no doubt: this crate was my long-lost mother's grave.

I moaned with grief, stumbling away from my gruesome discovery.

I needed to feel something, to cry … to scream … but,

once again, in that scary moment, I was frozen in time. My brain playing catch-up with its reality.

I took my cell phone out of my back pocket and dialed my Great Aunt Lane with shaky fingers.

As I stared into my mother's makeshift grave, eyes blurring with tears, I listened to the phone on the other end ring and ring and ring. Just as I was about to give up, I heard a thick cough on the other end and Lane's unmistakable husky smoker's voice: "Hello!"

"You. Fucking. Lied." I said, through clenched teeth, gripping the phone until my knuckles turned white.

Lane sighed noisily on the other end, as though she already knew what I was about to say. *Well, of course she did,* I realized. *She's known the truth all along.*

"What do you mean?" she asked, quietly.

The tremor was uncontrollable now, my entire body quivering. I tried to muster up the right words for my liar of an aunt.

"My mother hasn't been to visit you. There were no letters. No post cards … no fucking birthday cards…"

"What? Of course there were," Lane said, half-heartedly. But I could already hear the defeated tone of her voice…

"I know you're lying. Want to know how I know? Because I'm standing next to her dead body. And it's a skeleton, Lane! She's been here a long time…"

I heard Lane on the other line, taking in a sharp breath.

"Why did you cover for him, huh? How long have you known the truth?" I demanded, gripping the phone till my knuckles went numb. "Hell, maybe you even helped him. You always hated my mother."

I could remember hearing my mother say it: that my dad's family never liked her. But Lane had always been my father's favorite aunt. He talked about her so fondly that there were times I often wondered why we didn't go see her more often ... but as I grew older, I understood. Mom didn't feel welcome.

"Listen, Natalie. Your mama..."

"My mama what?" I shrieked, defensively.

"She killed that girl. The one in the field."

My heart lurched in my chest. "Excuse me?"

"Listen here. She did it to protect your brother. That Jenny girl was crazy, nuts ... claiming your brother had raped her."

I gasped, for the first time connecting it with Chrissy's version of events. *She didn't want to steal Jack, she wanted to destroy him...*

"The night your daddy called me, asking me to take in Jack for a while ... I never questioned it. Not then, and not later either ... I knew something was up, especially after I saw what happened in the papers ... but I wasn't sure which one of them did it. I didn't know it was her. And your brother, when he finally found out the truth, about what your mama did ... I guess he thought she had to pay for it. I was the only one he told, you know. I'm the only one he could trust."

"Yeah, because you lied for him!" I screamed over the roaring of the storm outside, and the one deep in my chest.

"You know your father ... he couldn't handle that sort of thing. I don't think he wanted to know the truth, honestly. He skirted around it. Told me to tell you that your mother was fine to make you feel better ... but he knew. Deep down he had to know what Jack had done. Because your mama would never just up and leave. She thought she'd go to prison one day, yes ... but she never would have abandoned you all."

"My mother wouldn't kill Jenny ... and Jack wouldn't kill his own mother," I moaned, staring at the evidence right in front of me. Mom told me ... said she might be going away for a while ... *was she trying to warn me that she might one day be arrested for killing Jenny? Or was she telling me she planned to leave town for good...?*

"There was an incident when your mom arrived home from work that day; Jenny was there waiting when she pulled in. She followed your mom inside, making chit chat, and then announced that Jack had raped her. Said she was going to the cops and there was nothing anyone could do to stop her. Jack was upstairs asleep, you see ... my sweet boy. He never even knew about the confrontation."

This isn't real. This isn't real. Please tell me this isn't real.

Lane continued, "And your mother ... well, she was boiling water for noodles when she told her. And your mama, always so impulsive, she was ... she freaked. Tossed that pot of boiling water right at her. She had to finish the job after that ... you know, there was no coming back after..."

Crime scene photos flashed before my eyes. Those burn marks on Jenny's face... I imagined her holding up her hands to protect herself, boiling hot water striking her hands and cheeks...

"Your mama did it for Jack. That girl would have ruined his life, Natalie. She killed her there, you know. After the burns, Jenny tried to run. But your mama chased her. Ended up right out there in the barn with a kitchen knife...she choked and stabbed her to death. Didn't know how else to stop her! And after she realized what'd she done, she used a wheelbarrow to push her. Left that stupid girl in the middle of the field. That girl never should have told lies ... if Jenny wasn't lying about your brother, then she never would have died ... she backed your mama into a corner. "

"But Chrissy..." I said, mind spinning as I tried to imagine my mother in the dark, pushing a dead girl's body through the field. *The mother I knew could never do that ... could she?!*

Lane was still talking. "Oh, don't feel sorry for that stupid Chrissy bitch either ... that girl was dumb enough to admit to it. And your mother snuck in and planted the shoes for good measure; for once she had some brains about her. She didn't like those two together. Your brother was too good for a Cornwall. Let's face it. Being a Cornwall, she was probably headed to jail anyway. Your mama just put her on the fast track there. Honestly, when your parents told me what happened, and explained that your mother was protecting Jack ... well, that was the first time I actually respected your mother. At least she protected her own. That's a mother's job, you know. Or, I guess you wouldn't know that, would you?"

Now that Lane was talking, all I wanted to do was make her shut the hell up.

"My sweet Jack ... he had no idea your mother killed her. Like everyone else in town, he believed it was his little trashy girlfriend that did it. And I sure as hell wasn't planning to tell him, or anyone else for that matter. I would have taken that secret to my grave, just like your daddy did. But it was your mama herself who told him. Chrissy had been convicted and she was off the hook. But your mother finally admitted the truth to Jack, thinking your brother would be grateful that she protected him from a rape charge. But he was still hung up on that girl ... the men in our family don't pick them well, do they? I don't think Jack meant to kill your mother ... he was just so shocked, and angry. And pissed at your mama for letting Chrissy go down for the crime. When I heard he killed himself on the anniversary of your mother's death, it ate me up with grief ... he should have just moved on like it never happened. But I guess, in the end, he had that weakness in him, just like you and your mother. He always was a pure, kind soul..."

My mother never left me. *She never left...*

In my mind, I rewound the clock ... seeing her face, the

worried look in her eye leading up to those days before she "left". *She thought she was going somewhere ... jail, possibly. But she never expected my brother to kill her. My mother's been dead since I was fourteen. All this time, she's been here ... right here ... under my feet. I felt her ... I never stopped feeling her presence here on the farm.*

The barn was spinning, the shadows playing tricks on my eyes ... the phone fell to the barn floor with a shattering thud.

I stumbled around several steps, then fell to my knees. Somewhere in the distance, I could still hear Lane's croaky voice, trying to shout to me through the phone ... but all I could see was my mother stuffed in that hellish trunk...

I forced myself back on my feet and barreled through the heavy barn doors.

In the marshy field, I stared up at the sky as a tunnel of rain hammered down on me. Lightning cracked the sky, thunder rocking the ground.

I screamed at no one and everyone, the rattling horror in my voice echoing through the empty field and bouncing back and forth through the trees ... spreading like a storm through the entire town of Austin.

Chapter Thirty-Three

They say that the truth will set you free. But sometimes truth *is* the prison.

My truth ... the truth of my family's lies ... has created its own little prison inside me. I set out to write a book, Chrissy's biography and detailed version of her crime. Instead, it turned out to be a memoir—the story of my own family's legacy, and how little white lies evolved into a decades-long web of suffering.

It's no longer her story to tell. *It's mine.*

I ask Chrissy often: *when are you going to sue the state for sending you to prison when you were innocent?*

She always counters with: *when are you going to write that book?*

That shuts me up really quick.

Because the truth is, I could write the story and people would probably read it. There will always be people who need to hear the details of other people's pain, and I can't say I blame them. I've had offers from other writers to do it, asking if they can write my family's story...

But, for some reason, I keep telling them no.

Because that's the thing about the truth: it's harder to tell than lies. Especially when it's an ugly truth like mine.

It's not that I don't love writing. I still want to write a book someday. But I'm thinking about something fun— maybe a rom-com or a western.

Something so far from the truth that I can almost believe the lie.

Once again, the Breyas farm is littered with pieces of crime tape. Only this time they're on the inside as well as the out. The blood inside the barn was too degraded for DNA testing, but luminol revealed a gory scene on the walls of the barn.

I'd like to say my mother was doing what she had to, protecting her own ... but now I'm questioning everything about who she was ... who they all were.

The knife she used to kill Jenny Juliott was buried in the trunk alongside her. I'd hoped for more ... a note from Jack inside her tomb, some type of explanation...

But his suicide spoke for itself—he killed our mother when he learned the truth, but he never recovered from his own monstrous actions.

Lane was arrested on a sunny Sunday afternoon for her role in the murder. She may not have been directly involved in the killings, but she was responsible for covering them up. I doubt she'll get much time because of her age, but it only seems fair to Jenny's family that she answer for her role in the murder.

The townspeople flock to Chrissy now, eager to give their condolences. Their "I always suspected you didn't do it" pats on the back. And the town is coming alive again, the old fears subsiding, as though there's no longer evil in the world now that my mother and brother are dead.

Now I'm the leper, crowds of people parting like the Red Sea when they see me coming. I don't think they blame me, exactly, but I think I make them uncomfortable. Surprisingly, Adrianna has been one of my biggest supporters, offering me a place to stay while the cops tore the farm apart.

I considered burying Mom next to Dad and Jack in the family plot. But doing that felt wrong. She'd spent enough time underground … I wanted her to soar for a while. She was cremated, her ashes tossed off the bridge over the Ohio River, a place she took me fishing once. It was a lovely day and although we hadn't caught anything, it was one of the best days of my life. I hope it was one of hers too.

Her body was so badly decomposed that the cause of death was undetermined. I hope that however he did it, it was quick and painless. I hope she didn't see it coming. Even though she did a terrible thing, I miss her. Somehow, knowing the truth—that she was a killer—hurts less than the thought that she abandoned me. Which is really fucked up, I know.

There are days when I wish I had never sent that letter to Chrissy. That I never would have unearthed these ugly old truths ... but now that feeling inside me—the one that always felt so unresolved—has faded. The truth might be its own version of prison, but at least I know the walls ... there's no more baggage left hanging, nothing unresolved to deal with.

When I went away to college, I was focused on the future. And in Austin, I was firmly stuck in the past.

Now all I want to do is start over, in a town where no one knows my name, and keep my feet firmly planted in the present.

I accepted a job at a bookstore in West Virginia—the pay is shit but the store looks amazing, and there's a cute little apartment complex nearby. I've never seen the mountains, but I want to.

Unlike me, Chrissy has decided to stay in Austin after all. So, she is staying and I'm going—a strange ending to it all, I guess.

But there's something thrilling about untangling myself from those deadly roots, letting myself go free...

Chrissy promised to stay in touch. I made no promises in return.

And Officer Nash, one of the few other people in town who has stood by me, has asked if he can come visit me some time in West Virginia. I told him that I would like that, but again, no promises made.

I left town with very little on a Wednesday afternoon. A tiny pack of clothes and toiletries. My car. Some cash I made from selling the farm.

And my mother's locket around my neck; a picture of me on one side, my brother Jack on the other.

For a while, we had it all. Before lies tore us apart...

When I get to West Virginia, I'll still be myself. Mostly. My personality will stay the same but I'm changing my name.

One last little white lie won't kill me—hopefully.

THE END

Don't miss *Whisper Island*, the next unputdownable thriller by Carissa Ann Lynch...

It was the perfect place to escape to.

It was the perfect place to die.

Get your copy today!

The One Night Stand

BY CARISSA ANN LYNCH

Now read on for an exclusive excerpt from *The One Night Stand*…

A night she won't forget…

When single mum Ivy wakes up to a complete stranger lying next to her, she knows her one night stand hook-ups have to stop. The encounters mean nothing to her, but for just a short time, they allow her to forget.

A murder she can't remember…

But then Ivy discovers the stranger in her bed has been stabbed to death, and she is covered in his blood…

The One Night Stand: Chapter 1

NOW

When I think about Delaney, I think about Dillan.

Three pounds, two ounces. The delivery nurse held her out to me in the palm of her hand, like a baby bird in its mother's nest. And right on cue, my tiny fowl opened her eyes and mouth, changing my life forever.

She's alive. Delaney is going to live, I'd thought.

But in those beady black eyes, those chirpy pink lips … I still saw the son who didn't make it: Dillan.

There's Delaney, but no Dillan.

A painful dichotomy of intense love and exceptional grief arose and gave birth to me that day.

"Only one twin survived." The doctor was soft-spoken and honey blonde; I'll never forget the contours of her face.

And those words ... her words would haunt me for the next fifteen years, probably longer. There was a name for my tragedy: twin-to-twin transfusion syndrome. In layman's terms, she had described it as one twin donating blood to the other. But the way she described it was almost morbid – one twin sucking up all the nutrients, sucking the life right out of its roommate...

My beautiful Delaney was headstrong and iron-willed, and it didn't surprise me that she was the stronger of the two.

So, when I woke up to find my fifteen-year-old daughter standing over me, her eyes like shiny black marbles glowing in the moonlit shadows of my room, the first thing I thought about was Dillan.

Even now, Dillan is still one of my first thoughts each morning. I wonder what he would have looked like, as a teenager. Maybe just like Delaney, with black feathery hair and deep brown eyes. If you take away the lashes, and the girlish curve of her jaw ... I can almost see what my son would have been...

"Mom!" Delaney hissed, tugging the blankets from my chest. It was the hiss that did it – a warning sign, that Delaney was about to scream, or in the very least, get angry and throw a few things.

"W-What is it, honey? What time is it?"

My eyes fought to stay open, my contact lenses that I wasn't supposed to sleep in at night, sticking to the backs of my eyelids.

Delaney stood up straight, her skin so pasty and pale that it was almost translucent in the low-lit room. She had this funny look on her face.

I know that look.

Not anger, which was her go-to emotion these days … not sadness, which was probably the runner-up. No, not either of those.

Delaney is scared, I realized with a start, sitting up too fast, my head swimming as I reached for her.

"What's wrong, Laney?"

But Delaney's eyes refused to meet mine; they were trained on something else beside me…

"There's a stranger in your bed." Her words were like shivery little whispers in the dark.

My scalp prickled with fear and I leapt from the bed, nearly knocking her backwards. I stared at the shape of a man lying on the usually empty side of my bed.

He had long legs, so long they were hanging over the end of the bed. Hairy toes poked out from beneath the blankets.

I took a small step closer, holding my breath.

He was buried beneath the sheets, except for his gangly toes and a few blond pokes of hair pricking out from the top…

My brain tried to play catch up with what my eyes were seeing, but Delaney cut in, "Who the hell is he?" She took the words straight out of my mouth.

No longer was she that scared little girl I remembered from her youth – she had transitioned back into her usual mood: angry at times, and don't-give-a-fuck mostly.

"I have no idea, Laney."

It wasn't a lie, not exactly. I had no recollection of inviting anyone over, but it wasn't the first strange man I'd had in my bed this month...

"Nice, Mom. Real nice," Delaney groaned.

My mind raced, thoughts trickling back to the last thing I remembered… I'd been online again, that stupid dating site. I hadn't wanted a profile in the first place, but Pam and Jerry, my two friends from work, had set the whole thing up for me.

Did I invite one of the guys I met online to come over to the house last night? Was I drinking again? Is that why I can't remember?

Suddenly, it was starting to make sense: I rarely drank alcohol, not until recently, and not since my early twenties. If I'd had a few beers last night, or even a little wine, then maybe … maybe I had blacked out completely.

But a quick scan of the room revealed no empty cans or bottles. No evidence that I'd been drinking at all.

How could I be so irresponsible? What the hell was I thinking, inviting a man over with my teenage daughter across the hall?

"Go back to bed. I'll wake him up and ask him to leave."

When Delaney didn't budge, I raised my voice a few octaves: "You have school in the morning. Now, go!"

The hurt expression on her face came and went so quickly, I almost wondered if I'd imagined it. A flutter of guilt rose up. Delaney wasn't a child anymore; I often had to remind myself of that. I shouldn't scold her so harshly; rather, I should try to talk to her like an equal, I thought, regretfully.

"Screw you," she huffed, then turned and marched out of the room. The door to my bedroom slammed bitterly behind her.

My eyes drifted back to the lumpy man. I'd been expecting him to wake up after Laney's outburst, but he was still sleeping peacefully.

In the silence of my bedroom, I crept over to the window and sat down on my favorite reading bench that overlooked our suburban street. My head felt groggy and strange, and I waited for the details of last night to come into focus…

I pressed my head against the windowpane and sighed. It was almost morning, the dark mountain ridges in the distance tipped with dusty browns and burgundy reds.

How long has it been since I watched the sun rise?

When Delaney was young, she'd loved the outdoors. But I had still been with her father then, Michael. Most of my memories of her early years were corrupted by memories of fights with Michael and sleepless nights as I grieved over Dillan.

Here's the thing: when you bring a baby home from the hospital, you're supposed to be happy. "It's a miracle that even one of the twins survived," the doctor had told me. "At least you have Delaney," my friends had told me.

But having a beautiful baby girl didn't make me any less sad about the son I'd lost, the room with blue borders I'd never use, the drawers of blankets and the onesies I'd picked out specifically for him… They were all still waiting for me when I came back home from the hospital. Some things couldn't be forgotten, even if I did love Delaney with all my heart.

Michael left us when Delaney was five. Unfortunately, he didn't go far.

Less than two miles from here, he lived with his new wife, Samantha, and baby sons, Braxton and Brock, in a Victorian mansion they had restored. Delaney had a room there – she *loved* that room – and she visited them every weekend.

Apparently, Michael's not verbally abusive with his new family, and he gave up drinking years ago… How convenient for them.

The drinking and the dating – I'd only started that recently, with the nudging insistence of my two best friends. It seemed good for me – healthy, even – but incidents like this couldn't happen.

Meeting up with strange men, bringing them to my home … not a good example for Delaney. And probably not safe either.

I had no recollection of what had happened last night, or who this strange man was. This went way beyond normal socializing – I'd obviously blacked out completely.

I moved to another window, this one front-facing, and peered out through the blinds at the street in front of our house.

My Dodge minivan was parked at the curb, crooked as usual. But tonight, there was a navy-blue Camaro parked behind it, and I knew it didn't belong to my neighbor. *It has to be his*, I thought, glancing back at the hairy set of toes.

Well, at least this mystery man drives a nice car. I've dated worse...

If only I could remember who he was or what we did last night...

"Excuse me." I tiptoed over to the bed.

I poked his shoulder area, and when he didn't budge, I pushed the blankets away from his face. His face was smooth, eyes closed. He looked downright peaceful.

Damn, I wish I slept that soundly.

"I need you to go. I don't mean to be rude, but I think I had too much to drink last night. I don't usually let guys stay overnight. And my daughter ... well, she has school in the morning. So, can you please head home?"

But the strange man didn't respond. No breathy snores, not even a slight twitch. No movement, whatsoever...

"Excuse me!" I knew I was being a bitch, but I didn't care. My daughter had just discovered a strange man in my bed. My daughter who was already having enough troubles lately...

Since joining the dating site, I'd invited a couple men over, but only when Delaney was at her dad's. Inviting a stranger from the internet to my house on a school night while Delaney was home...well, that was totally out of character for me.

But lately, I hadn't been acting like myself at all.

I need this man out of my bed... Right now.

I placed both hands on his chest and gave him a sturdy shake. "Wake up, please."

When he still didn't react, I grew frustrated. Gripping the plain white sheet in my left fist, I tugged it the rest of the way off.

"Jesus!"

I leapt back from the bed, shaky hands covering my mouth and nose.

The mystery man was completely naked, but that wasn't the shocking part. It was the dark purple stain in the center of his abdomen.

And beneath him...

"Oh. Oh..." The floor beneath my feet became watery and strange, the walls spinning like a tilt-o-whirl. My backside made sharp contact with the dresser behind me and a picture fell to the floor with a sickening thud.

Holding my mouth so I wouldn't scream and alert Delaney, I tiptoed like a demented ballerina, back over to the edge of the bed.

I pulled on the light string, lighting up the room to see him better.

I bit down on my fingers, muffling the terror that threatened to burst from within me...

The stranger's face looked peaceful enough: eyes and mouth closed; hands flat at his sides. But he was rigid, *too rigid* … almost like he was laying inside a casket instead of my bed.

It might as well be a casket…

Because he's dead as fuck, I realized in horror.

I bit down harder, my body trembling in fear.

I moved in as close as I dared, nervously studying his wound. It was a hole above his belly button, jagged and red, with a dry purple stain blooming out like a flower around it. Dry streaks of blood stained both sides of his waist from where he'd bled out in the bed beside me.

The sheet beneath him was stained dark red with blood, so red it was almost purple.

So much blood!

It had probably soaked all the way through the mattress and box springs. There was blood on my side too. Realization sinking in, I looked down at my own blue nightdress.

No way would I have let a man see me in this old, worn-out gown. So, why am I wearing it? Nothing about this makes sense.

How the hell did he get here? And who the fuck is he?!

Tentatively, I dabbed at a big, crusty stain on the side of my gown. The color of the gown was too dark to tell, but I knew without a doubt it was blood.

His blood.

He'd been bleeding in the bed beside me … and I'd had no idea.

Vomit tickled the back of my throat, hot and acrid.

How the hell did he get here in the first place?

And, most importantly, how did he wind up dead?

The One Night Stand: Chapter 2

NOW

Delaney had no idea that there was a dead man in my bed – not just dead, *murdered*. I'd changed my clothes, locked my bedroom door behind me, and gone to the bathroom to take a quick shower.

And when Delaney woke up at 7am for school, I was standing in the kitchen with a cup of coffee in my hands, a bowl of oatmeal and a glass of orange juice sitting on the table for her.

Most mornings were chaotic, me getting ready for work, both of us rushing out the door at the same time. But everything about today was different.

I have a feeling life will be very different from now on.

"I take it you're not going to work?" Delaney said, shuffling into the kitchen. She had on a thick black hoodie and fashionably ripped jeans, even though it was supposed to be a warm day for fall. I fought the impulse to ask her to go change. She wasn't ten anymore – I couldn't pick out her clothing, as much as I would have liked to.

"I'm going in late today because I have an important meeting in the afternoon. So, my schedule is a little different." The lie flowed from my tongue like honey.

I wasn't scheduled to work late; in fact, I'd left a shaky message for my boss telling him I had a stomach virus, which isn't completely a lie.

Finding a murdered man in your bed does have the tendency to make you a little queasy...

But I'd already missed a couple days recently; not only could I not afford another day off, but my job could be on the line.

"Right. So, ya gonna tell me who he is, or not?" Delaney demanded, globs of oatmeal swishing around her mouth as she talked. She lifted her cup of juice to her stained red lips, glanced down into the cup with a look of disgust, then slammed it back down.

I wonder what they serve for breakfast at Michael's house, I thought, drearily. Probably crepes and chocolate-chip waffles ... made from scratch by Wife #2, of course.

I took a seat in the chair across from her. "He's just a friend, honey."

My voice was so calm, so smooth... I almost didn't recognize it.

"What—the fuck—ever." Delaney pushed the chair back with a caw-like screech, and I winced.

"Please don't talk to me that way. I'm a grown woman and I'm allowed to date if I want to. Your father has certainly moved on."

Instantly, I regretted bringing Michael and Samantha into this.

Delaney left the kitchen without another word.

I heard the jangling of her backpack slipping over her shoulders in the hall, and seconds later, the screen door thumped shut behind her. There were days when the closest I came to understanding my daughter was trying to interpret the shuffle of her feet and the velocity with which she closed her bedroom door.

I remained at the table, clutching my cup of coffee. I heard the squeaky air brakes of the bus pulling up outside. I closed my eyes, waiting for the bus to get all the way to the end of the road before I moved.

When I couldn't hear it anymore, I stood up.

Finally, I could allow myself to be shaky and afraid.

How could I be so stupid? And what am I going to do?

Obviously, I hadn't killed the man. I didn't have a violent bone in my body.

But that hasn't always been the case, has it? I scolded myself.

Is it possible? Could I have blacked out and hurt someone?

But that red-rose hole in his stomach... It looked like a

knife wound, a deep one that took a lot of strength. And anger.

I shuddered.

And if he were mentally unstable, why would he choose to take his own life in a strange woman's bed after sex, and why would he do it that way…?

And I hadn't seen a weapon… If he'd done it to himself, there would be a weapon…

"Holy shit. What am I going to do?" I said aloud, the fear in my voice finally matching the terror inside me.

I carried the mug over to the kitchen sink and washed it, nearly dropping it a dozen times. Out the window above the sink, I could see my neighbor, Fran, in the street. She was fetching her mail, one arm in a cast. I waved but she didn't see me.

She had stopped, mail-in-hand, and she was staring at something. I followed her line of sight…she was looking at the sporty blue car parked behind mine. She turned her head and looked straight at me, eyes narrowing.

"Shit, shit, shit…"

I waited for her to turn around with her mail and wobbled back inside her own house.

The house was eerily quiet with Delaney gone, almost like a mausoleum. I wasn't used to being here during the day, and it felt wrong somehow, seeing the early morning shadows reflecting off the dusty bookshelves and cheap Ikea furniture.

Well, I guess it kind of is like a crypt, considering there's a dead man locked up in my bedroom…

Every time I closed my eyes, each blink, each second, I could see his moon-white face, the rosy red stain on his abdomen … the congealed blood staining my mattress and sheets.

My phone buzzed in my pocket, startling me more than it should have. I yelped, then took it out, hands quivering as I opened a new text message.

I was expecting a reply from my boss. I'd left a hoarse, whispery message for him, thankful at the time that he hadn't answered. But sooner or later, I'd have to talk to him…

But the message was from Delaney.

I think I'll stay at Dad's again tonight. Sam and I are going to finish the library mural. Plus, this will give you and your new friend more time together!

I could imagine her glaring out the bus window, jaw flexing in anger, her phone clutched like a weapon in her hand. Was she being nice or sarcastic?

Definitely the latter, I decided.

Every single word was like a dagger … and I had no doubt that was her intention. She'd been angry with me every day for the past year, sometimes for a reason, but mostly not. *Teenagers are supposed to be angry, right?* I had just assumed this was normal, a part of the growing process …

but I was wrong about that. Delaney was going through a lot more than the average teen.

It was a weekday – not her dad's night to take her.

Would she explain to him why she wanted to stay with him again? What will he think about the man in my bed…?

And every time she called her stepmom *Sam*, I tasted bile in the back of my throat.

But none of this really matters right now, does it? Because I have a bigger crisis to tend to.

I knew Delaney was expecting a big reaction, for me to put up a fight…

Okay, honey. Have fun.

I typed back. I almost considered writing, 'Send Sam my love', but I knew Delaney would see right through it.

She gets her snarky humor from me, I guess.

For a split second, I could almost believe it was a normal Tuesday – dealing with Delaney's attitude and my own bitterness over Michael – but nothing about this day was normal: a murdered man was in my room.

In my bed.

Slowly, I made my way down the short, skinny hallway, breathing in through my nose and out through my mouth. I stopped in front of the bathroom door. On my tiptoes, my fingers reached for the slim, gold key that I kept on the ledge of the door frame; a master key to all the rooms in the house.

I gripped the key so tight in my right palm that it burned.

Finally, I used it to unlock my bedroom door and I stepped inside.

There was a part of me, a silly, stupid part, that hoped —*prayed*—that the body in my bed would no longer be there.

But in the light of day, the strange man still looked dead as ever.

I locked the door behind me even though I was home alone, and, noiselessly, I crept over to the bed. The sheets were hanging halfway off from where I'd tugged on them earlier. I went ahead and pulled them completely away from the bed and laid them in a crumpled pile by the door.

Shaking, I could barely breathe as I approached the naked man.

Who are you? How did you get in my bed? And most importantly, who stabbed you?

His face was wrinkle-free and hairless.

He can't be much older than thirty, I realized, finally getting a good look at him in the light of the day.

There was no jewelry on his body. No wedding ring on his finger. His fingernails and toenails were neatly trimmed, like someone who took care of himself. But, then again, not someone who would necessarily stand out from the crowd: his hair was sandy brown, his face plain, his body average…

277

This man is a complete stranger to me. I've never seen him before, not a day in my life…not on the dating site, nowhere…

I'd been talking regularly to a few men online, but this guy wasn't one of them. New potential matches messaged daily, but I wouldn't have invited him over without at least getting to know him a little bit, would I? But then I remembered the last guy I'd had over…I hadn't known him well either.

Every man I'd talked to and dated over the last month came rushing back all at once, their faces merely profile pictures, flipping one by one in my mind…

Swipe, swipe, swipe.

And why don't I remember what happened last night?

I forced myself to move closer, to study the features of his face…

Nearly two hours had passed since Delaney shook me awake. In that short span of time, the man's body had turned even stiffer. His eyes were still closed but his lips were parted. For a moment, I waited, expecting those lips to move, to tell me *'it's all a dream, go back to bed silly'*…

But nothing happened.

I should call the cops.

Why hadn't I called them already?

Because it almost seems too late to do that now, a voice inside me warned.

I imagined me telling the police the truth: *I was scared. Freaked out. I didn't know what to do. So, I waited until my daughter left for school before I called you.*

No, officers, I have no idea who he is. No, I don't remember how he got here. Of course I didn't kill him! I imagined myself saying.

I couldn't call them until I could explain how he got here ... and until I could describe what transpired last night before he ended up in my bed and ended up ... dead.

But that wasn't the only reason for my hesitation. *Michael.* If he found out about this, if he found out the truth about me ... he would try to take Delaney away from me, permanently. He'd been doing it for years now, wearing the face of a dutiful father whenever she was around, then morphing into his old self alone with me. Nothing about the man had changed, but according to his new wife, he was perfect.

Perfect, my ass...

He wanted Delaney all to himself. That way he could have his whole, perfect family and erase me from existence completely. If he found out about this, about all of it ... well, he'd probably try to get full custody for sure. Not probably – he would.

I know he would.

And the scary part: *I don't even know if Delaney would mind.*

Sure, we had our good days. But what about all the bad ones? Over the last two weeks, she'd spent more time with her other family than with me...

I imagined the cops cuffing me and carting me off to jail, Delaney sneering from the driveway, Michael smiling victoriously. And Wife #2 beside him, with her plaster-perfect smile, waving me off as they took me away...

I scurried around the room, diverting my eyes from the dead man, searching for his clothes or wallet. Something to help identify him.

I may not remember what happened, but I know I must have met him online.

A pair of dark brown chinos and a flimsy old flannel lay messily on the floor beside my dresser. No underwear. No shoes...?

That doesn't make sense.

I dug through the pockets of his chinos—no keys either. And no wallet.

This is insane! Did I pick up a homeless man off the street, or what?

But then I remembered the navy-blue Camaro sitting outside my house. It had to belong to him. There was no one else around it could belong to.

Rubbing my cheeks, panic surged through my veins as I tried to trace my way back in my mind...

Did he drug me? Is that why I don't remember?

My head did feel groggy and strange, although that could be from a hangover... And if a stranger had showed up and tried to rape me, I would have tried to defend myself. I didn't have any wounds on my hands, or the rest of my body.

And if it had been consensual sex...

I know how my body feels after sex and this isn't it.

I wasn't sore or achy. I didn't feel violated or injured in anyway. In fact, I didn't feel like I'd had sex at all. And the old gown I'd had on when I woke up…it was the least sexy thing I owned. I couldn't see myself putting that ratty old thing on for anyone, much less a man I'd invited over for the first time and planned to sleep with…

I carried the man's clothes over to the pile of bedding and, shakily, dropped them to the floor. I scooped up a pair of my own jeans and a t-shirt which I'd been wearing yesterday, I remembered. The last thing I remember was fighting with Delaney.

But what happened after we fought?

She slammed her bedroom door the way she usually does, I recalled.

Then I folded laundry and made dinner. I yelled for her to come out of her room. And by the time she did, the chicken was cold. We barely ate or talked. Another silent war between us, which was all too typical for us these days – a constant battle, and one I lost more days than most.

She'd been texting furiously while she sat at the table and when I asked her who she was chatting with, she'd said, "My father", with such viciousness it had made my blood run cold.

And after dinner she'd gone back to her room and I'd gone back to mine, I remembered. On school nights, we usually went to be early, around ten or eleven or so.

But I didn't go straight to bed last night, I remembered.

I'd got online. Checked my dating profile for new

messages. It was a great way to escape, and for the first time in years, I'd started feeling attractive – *wanted* – again.

I do remember getting on the site last night. But what happened after…?

I spotted a pair of purple panties—my panties—on the floor by my side of the bed. I hated to get close to the dead guy again, but I went over to retrieve them anyway.

I gripped the underwear in a ball in my hand and forced myself to get down on my knees on the floor.

I have to check under the bed. But what if there's a knife under there? What if it's covered in blood…?

There's no such thing as monsters under the bed. I could remember saying that to Delaney countless times when she was little.

When she still needed her mother. When she still looked up to me and thought my word was gold.

Trembling, I crouched on the floor beside the bed and pressed my face to the matted carpet.

Monsters under the bed…why does that age-old fear never fully disappear with time?

I squinted into the dark, narrow gap between my bed and the floor.

I gasped and stumbled back as I came face to face with, not the murder weapon, but … another corpse.

Only this one wasn't a stranger.

The One Night Stand: Chapter 3

BEFORE

How did it begin?

I guess it started the way most bad things do: with secrets.

And then, of course, there were also the lies.

Lies that tasted like malt vinegar, but flowed like syrup from our tongues ... and what was the truth anymore? I don't think we'd recognize it if it were staring us straight in the face...

"Laney, are you ready?" I dropped my purse with a smack on the entryway floor, just like I did every day after work. I was exhausted. Most days I'd take a shower and throw together something for dinner then fall asleep watching TV.

But then I remembered: Samantha was coming.

I scooped my purse off the floor and carried the bulgy black bag to my bedroom.

Our house wasn't exactly a penthouse – paint peeling, the original lime green from the 60s playing peek-a-boo through the cracks. But it was clean (mostly) and roomy for just the two of us. Two bedrooms, two baths. Our furniture wasn't fancy, but it was comfortable. I liked to think of our small bungalow as "homey"; it was also small enough to keep us together and large enough to keep us from killing each other…

I kept the house tidy; well, I thought I did…but now that I knew Samantha was coming – or *Sam* as Delaney liked to call her – the house was bathed in a whole new light.

I swept the living room curtains back, a cloud of dust tickling my nose and the back of my throat. The windows were grimy, a thin layer of dust coating the sills and every baseboard in sight.

And the air in our house…today, it felt stale and muggy.

A pile of unpaid bills lay cluttered on the arm of the sofa from where I'd forgotten to finish sorting through them last night.

The kitchen was worse. Breakfast dishes and coffee mugs were stacked on the counter, and the drain in the sink was giving off that putrid egg smell again…

Most days, I left for work by seven, with Delaney not far behind. There was rarely time to tidy up in the mornings, which was why I often saved all that for after work.

Leaving the dishes, I drifted back to the living room, my chest tightening with dread. In addition to the dust and messy mail pile, there were empty bottles of tea and

Vitamin Water crowding the coffee table. Delaney had been watching *Teen Mom 2* last night when I'd taken myself to bed.

When did she stop using the garbage can? I thought, angrily.

It's like you spend their early years teaching them every day common tasks and social skills, and just when you think they've mastered them, you have to re-instruct them as teens.

I stuffed the bunch of mail between two couch cushions and scooped up Delaney's mess in my arms. When I went to throw it away, I realized the garbage was full. Not only that, it smelled like last night's fettucine.

And the carpet, has it always looked this dingy?

It had been needing to be replaced since … well, since the day we moved in nine years ago. But replacing carpet was one of those costly projects that I planned for tax return season but never got around to. Because there was always something else that came up – tires for the minivan, new school clothes for Delaney, a broken hot water heater, a busted drum in the dryer…

It was Friday, and in our house, Fridays meant *Michael*.

Usually, Delaney's friend Viola dropped her at Michael's after school. But ever since I'd discovered the pot stash in her top drawer, Delaney had been riding the bus as part of her punishment.

I wasn't sure if her friends were bad influences, exactly, but I knew that not getting to ride with them to and from school might make Delaney think twice before picking up another joint.

Or it will make her better at hiding it, I considered, pressing down on the tender spot between my eyes and praying another migraine wasn't on its way.

I'd offered – a few times – to take Delaney to Michael's. Michael and his new wife's house was close, and it would take me less than a half hour to take her there, after work. But Samantha – or *Sam* – had insisted on picking her up this week. "It's no trouble, no trouble at all," she'd said in that high, silky voice of hers that I'd grown to detest. *'I don't work, so it's no bother. You shouldn't have to drive out here after working all day…'*

But even *that* felt like a sneaky dig – Samantha didn't work because she didn't have to. Michael's income was enough to sustain them.

Was she rubbing that in my face, or was I just being paranoid?

On the surface, Samantha seemed pleasant, polite, sweet even. But still…

No trouble at all, I thought warily, looking around at the mess I'd come home to.

"Delaney?" I shouted. Then, lowering my voice: "Are you ready in there? You should give me a hand out here."

I couldn't imagine *Sam* raising her voice, which should have made me feel better about Delaney spending so much time with her new stepmom, but there was something about her I couldn't put my finger on. Something in my gut that said she was phony.

Oh, big surprise, Ivy! You don't trust your husband's pretty new wife, the one he left you for. Join the ex-wives club, I scolded myself.

Back in my bedroom, I scraped my hair into a tight knot. I fought the urge to put on makeup.

I don't need to impress that bitch, I thought bitterly.

But I picked up a pair of tweezers and tugged on a wiry gray hair that had seemingly sprouted overnight on my right temple. My bed was still unmade from this morning, sheets and comforter tangled in a knot at the foot of the bed. I fought another urge – to crawl under the covers and live there.

Maybe I'll hide in here when she knocks, I considered. *Nobody's home…*

I left the room and closed the door behind me.

I'll deal with that mess later, I decided.

I shuffled down the dimly lit hallway. There was still no sign of Delaney.

I stopped in front of the bathroom and pressed my ear to the door. Water was running, and I could hear something else – the faint sound of Delaney humming while she took a shower. Ever since Delaney had started high school, she had started taking extra-long showers.

Her sweet, melancholic voice was indistinguishable from that of a child's. For a moment, I could almost believe that on the other side of this door was my daughter, my old daughter, the one who splashed and sang, who squealed for me to jump in the tub and join her.

No, that daughter had been replaced with a new one – the daughter who locks every door and sneaks stashes of pot into her bedroom drawers...

I rapped softly on the door, but didn't bother turning the knob – she always locked every single door behind her.

So secretive ... but that's the way of teenagers, isn't it? There's always some vulnerable, wounded part of themselves they feel like they have to tuck away and hide. The person they trust the most as a child becomes the last person on Earth they'd ever confide in...

The humming stopped for a split second, but then it started up again.

Ignoring me, as usual.

The tune she was humming sounded familiar.

Row, row, row your boat...

"Delaney." I knocked again, harder this time. "You need to finish up. Samantha's due here any minute. It's rude to be in the shower when you know someone is on their way to pick you up..."

I didn't wait for an answer because I knew there wouldn't be one.

Truth was, I was less worried about Delaney's rudeness than my discomfort with the idea of being stuck interacting with *Sam* while Delaney got her shit together.

I'd imagined this whole pick-up going more smoothly— Delaney standing by the front door with her backpack in hand and ready, the exchange between Sam and I polite, but brisk. *Very brisk.* Then I'd stand on the front porch and wave. "Have a good time, you two!" I imagined myself shouting, in that perfect, *non-jealous* way, that responsible co-parents do.

But that scenario wasn't going to happen.

Michael nor Samantha had been to our house in a couple years; the drop-offs and pick-ups always facilitated by me, or Delaney's friends. And I liked it that way—the last thing I needed was Michael's judgement—his eyes scanning every square inch of our small modest home.

At least it's Samantha coming, not him. But still ... I don't feel like I can trust her either. I always feel like I'm under a microscope, being judged.

It's a strange feeling, being watched and overlooked at the same time...

My feet were achy from work, but I refrained from kicking off my dress flats; instead, I got busy washing the sticky mugs from this morning, and I hauled the garbage out to the dumpster in the alley out back.

By the time my lovely daughter emerged from the bathroom, the kitchen was neat and organized, and I was working the vacuum back and forth over the carpet in the living room, humming a mindless tune of my own.

Samantha was late, which surprised me a little, but also came as a relief.

The house is looking pretty good now, if I must say so myself...

But when I looked up and saw my daughter's face, my insides turned cold. Delaney was gripping her cell phone in her hand, shaking like a leaf.

I kicked the vacuum off with my right foot and pulled the cord from the wall.

"What's going on?"

Delaney was wearing skin-tight maroon leggings with a stretchy black blouse. I'd never seen the outfit before – undoubtedly, a new gift from her father or stepmom. My daughter was painfully pretty, in that way all young people are, skin soft and youthful like putty. Her body and face undamaged by motherhood, or time. You'd think I'd be used to it by now, but even after fifteen years, the depth of my daughter's beauty always knocked me off guard.

People say we look alike, but I don't see it.

And she was wearing makeup, something new – a silky slip of gloss on her lips, reddish-brown shadow a strange contrast with her navy-blue eyes. However, her long black hair was still tangled and damp from the shower.

Something was wrong; there was a milky-white shade to her skin, and she was gnawing on her bottom lip, the way she used to do when she was young…

"Well, what is it? What's wrong?" I tried to suppress my annoyance. Another thing about Delaney since becoming a teenager: she was dramatic as hell and getting an answer out of her was like pulling teeth with a pair of chopsticks.

"It's Sam. There … well, there's been an accident."

And just like that, Delaney's woman-like façade

crumbled completely. Her nose wrinkled up and she reached for me, falling into my chest. I held her there, shock rolling through me.

Delaney was sobbing, her body rocking back and forth into mine.

"Oh my gosh. What kind of accident?" I whispered.

I rubbed her back in slow circles, soothing her at my breast, just as I had done when she was young and needed me. But this felt different, and for the life of me, I couldn't remember the last time I'd held her.

It's been years, I realized sullenly.

As I hugged her, I could feel her bones through her skin, no more baby fat. Overnight, she'd become sharp angles and blunt curves ... a total stranger to me.

When did she lose weight? And why haven't I noticed before now?

Delaney still hadn't answered. I felt desperate to know, but my heart ached as she shook and cried in my arms.

Could my husband's new wife be ... dead?

For a brief moment, I considered how that would make me feel, *really feel*. Sure, I resented Samantha, but dead?

No, I wouldn't wish that on anybody. Especially not someone my daughter's grown so fond of. Her happiness is more important than any resentment I feel toward Michael and Samantha.

But there was another part of me, that niggly fierce mother in me, that felt slightly pained by my daughter's strong reaction.

It must be bad.

"Shhh... I'm sure it will be okay." I stroked the top of Delaney's hair, breathing in the heady smell of her honey-scented shampoo.

Delaney pulled back with a surprised jerk, flustered. She wiped her face with the back of her hands, smoothed her rumpled hair into place.

She remembers who she is now. No longer a baby who cries in her mother's arms...

"Dad texted while I was in the shower. Sam was on the way to get me when someone ran a red light and hit the side of her Mercedes. She's being taken to University Hospital. Her neck is broken, and some other things... That's all I know."

"Oh my God, that sounds serious," I said, reaching for her. I wanted to hold her again, try to make it better ... but, this time, she side-stepped me. With her back pressed to the couch, Delaney took out her cell phone out and started punching keys. "I need to go to the hospital. I need to make sure she's okay. And Dad probably needs me too. He sounded very worried..."

"Yes, of course, we should go right now. Let me grab my purse and slide on my shoes, then I'll take you."

Moments later, we were buckling our seatbelts in the minivan and backing out of the driveway. Delaney twisted her hair into a tight, wet knot at the base of her skull that oddly resembled my own.

"I know you must be so worried, honey. Are you okay?" I reached over out of habit, ready to pat her knee.

"I'm fine," she snapped, inching her legs out of reach. She shifted her body towards the passenger's window, still struggling to smooth the frizzy, loose pieces of hair that poked out from the stubby bun.

Twenty minutes later, the glaring red lights of University Hospital came into view. I flicked my signal on and turned into the crowded lot.

"I'll park in the garage. We can take the elevator up—"

"No, just drop me in the front."

I tapped my brakes outside the emergency room entrance, hesitating.

"But we could get towed. It'll only take a moment to grab a spot, Laney. I'll be fast, I promise."

"Mom," Delaney whined, "just drop me in the front, okay? I'll call you in a little while with an update."

"Oh." I felt my cheeks growing warm. "You don't want me to come inside with you? I'm sure your dad wouldn't mind. I'm concerned for Samantha too…"

"The last thing Dad needs is an extra stressor, okay? I'll let you know how she's doing as soon as I can. And I think you're right; she's going to be okay."

"Yes, I'm sure she will," I said, still hearing the ring of that word 'stressor' in my ears.

Is that all I am to my ex now, an extra blip of stress in his busy radar of life?

I parked at the curb behind a row of flashing ambulances. I watched two paramedics, as they unloaded an elderly man out the back on a big, white gurney.

Delaney let herself out the passenger's side, not looking back or saying goodbye. I watched my daughter as she ran towards the entrance, joining up with two familiar faces at the door: my ex-sister-in-law, Fiona, and my ex-father-in-law, Joseph.

Glad to see they turned out for Samantha. They didn't even come to the hospital when Delaney and Dillan were born...

My face burned with shame.

I shouldn't be thinking of myself at a time like this. Samantha has been injured and my daughter's upset.

Joseph and Fiona glanced over at me, expressions stony. Then, pretending I didn't exist the way they always did, they looked away. I watched as Joseph wrapped a thick arm around Delaney's shoulders and led her inside the hospital. I waited for them to disappear through the revolving doors.

The sun was nearly gone, the sky an ominous indigo color. I made the slow drive home, not even bothering with the radio.

As I approached our subdivision, I flicked my high beams on to combat the fog. My thoughts were muddled and strange.

Will Samantha be okay? What if she's not? Will Delaney be alright? But then those questions swelled into darker ones: *Why is Delaney so distraught over her stepmom? And why is she always so impressed by her? Am I losing my daughter completely? And why am I so damned jealous?*

I could see it in Delaney's eyes when she talked about her stepmom – they lit up. *'Sam's such a talented painter. Sam has a moon and star tattoo on her back. Sam showed me how to mix paint properly...'*

Blah blah fucking blah.

But guilt fluttered back.

This is no time for being petty.

I wasn't normally the praying type, but I said a small prayer under my breath for Samantha.

When I pulled in, there was a red Miata parked in my driveway. Loud 90s rap music boomed from the speakers, seemingly shaking the entire block.

Good thing I only have one neighbor for miles.

I parked beside the Miata, smiling warily.

"There you are!" Pam squealed. My oldest friend – my *best* friend – was sitting in the driver's seat, blonde hair crispy with hairspray. When she smiled, I saw a smudge of bright red lipstick on her freshly whitened teeth. I motioned for her to turn down the radio.

"Sorry," she said, grinning wildly. But her manic smile evaporated when she saw the worried look on my face. I rolled my window down farther, then turned off the engine.

"Oh, Ivy. What's the matter?"

Unhooking my seatbelt, I leaned my seat back a little and took a deep breath.

There's something about being around my best friend that makes me want to lie down and relax, tell her all about my day like she's Sigmund Freud...

"Samantha had an accident on her way to pick up

Delaney. She's at the hospital. It's serious, apparently. She has a broken neck."

Pam's eyes widened. "And we're upset about this, right?"

"Fuck, Pam. Of course we are. Delaney's upset. They've gotten so close…"

Pam raised her eyebrows, in that *Are you okay with that?* sort of way I found annoying.

That's the bad thing about best friends: they always know the things you think but cannot say. And Pam knew my secrets better than anyone.

"I'm sure she'll be okay, but Laney was so upset. I just hope they're all okay. What are you doing here, anyway? Not that I'm not glad to see you…"

Pam and I worked together, but Fridays were usually her day off.

"I came to pick you up, silly. Did you really think I'd let you spend your birthday alone?" Pam patted the empty passenger's seat with a sly grin.

My birthday.

I'd nearly forgotten about it since this morning, not that birthdays were a big deal for me anymore. The fact that Delaney hadn't wished me happy birthday all day had hurt a little, but maybe she had been going to, until Samantha's accident?

When Delaney was little, she'd loved birthdays – the cake and the candles, the singing and the presents. Hell, even when it wasn't one of our birthdays, she'd hold pretend birthday parties with her dolls and stuffed animals. One year, I'd even bought her a big plastic cake to play with at Christmas…

"You're so sweet, but I can't go anywhere. I need to stick around in case Laney needs me. She might want me to come to the hospital…"

"Ivy," Pam said, sternly, "it's Michael's day to take care of her, and I'm sure she'll call you if she needs you. She's a big girl now, and we won't go far. Just down to the pub for dinner and drinks. Jerry's meeting us there, too."

"I'm still in my damn work clothes," I grunted, pointing at my faded green polo shirt.

Pam gave me a look.

I know that look.

She wouldn't take no for an answer.

"Okay, fine. At least let me go change real quick. But is it okay if I follow you down there instead of riding?" Pam was a heavy drinker at times – never a drunk – but she often drank a few too many when she went out. And lately, she went out a lot more than I did.

We hadn't gone "out" together in a long time, and I just felt safer driving myself.

"Just in case Laney calls while we're out. I want to be able to go and get her if I need to," I explained.

"Fine," Pam groaned, waving for me to hurry up and get ready.

Dinner and drinks with Pam and Jerry, my two best

friends – my *only* friends, really – sounded pretty good, actually.

Hell, you only turn forty once, right?

"I'll wait out here," Pam croaked, lighting a cigarette and blowing a big cloud of smoke in my direction. By the time I had my front door open, her music was blasting again.

The living room was dark, and I nearly tripped over the vacuum I'd left out earlier.

It took me a few minutes to pick out something to wear. Finally, I settled on a black pencil skirt and a silky red and black top that was getting tight around my waistline but still hugged my breasts just right. Then I combed my hair and brushed my teeth, strutting back outside. I forced myself to smile with all my teeth – mostly for Pam's benefit, but also in the hopes it would lift my own sour mood.

Pam was smoking another cigarette, looking down at the pink iPhone in her lap.

"Look okay?" I did a goofy spin in the driveway. Suddenly, the idea of being with Jerry and Pam instead of at home worrying by myself *did* sound kind of fun.

"You're gorgeous, Ivy. Don't look a day over thirty!" she teased.

"Oh, bullshit. But thanks. I'll be right behind you, but first, let me text Laney. I want to see how she's doing, see if she has any updates on Sam."

"Sam. When did you start calling her that?" Pam snorted.

I waved dismissively and took my phone out of my purse.

I was a little disappointed to see that Delaney hadn't messaged me with any news yet, but it had only been a half hour since I'd dropped her off.

I typed:

How is Sam doing? Call me if you need me and I'll be right there.

As soon as I clicked send, I heard a tiny ding coming from the passenger's side floorboard.

I was surprised to see Delaney's phone, a black Android with a bedazzled case lying face down on the floor.

She must have dropped it when she got out earlier…

Delaney guarded her phone like a precious jewel. Not uncommon for any teen, I guess.

I could remember tucking my pager away, hiding it between my mattress and box spring, but I'm not exactly sure who I was hiding it from since my parents were already dead by then…

I stared at the phone, sparkling in the hazy moonlight outside my window.

It wouldn't take Delaney long before she realized she'd left her phone behind, if she hadn't already.

Pam honked beside me and I yelped.

"Alright. Let's go," I groaned, shifting the van into gear.

My hands were clammy on the steering wheel as I squeezed between a truck and a Volvo in the back row of Midge's Bar and Grill. It was "our" spot – Pam, Jerry, and me – on those rare days when we were granted an extended lunch break. They had excellent salads and pasta bowls for lunch, but I'd never been here this late at night.

The parking lot was crowded with cars and the screeching sound of an electric guitar floated from the open deck that was normally closed in the daytime. Couples and groups were wandering through the parking lot, making their way inside.

I gave Delaney's phone on the floor one last, longing glance, then I took out my own phone and messaged Michael.

Delaney left her phone in the van. I thought she might be looking for it. If she needs me, will you have her give me a call from your cell, please?

I clicked send, then added one more text:

Wishing and praying for Samantha.

Reading it back, it looked corny. And maybe a little sarcastic. Would Michael believe me?

Probably not, I decided.

There was no love lost between us – well, not anymore. He knew I was angry and resentful, and I knew he didn't give a shit. He'd never apologized for cheating on me, not even once…

As I shimmied out of the van, I couldn't help noticing that everyone looked much younger, much prettier.

Is this what it feels like to get old?

A tiny knot of women – well, girls, really – slid past me, cell phones held out in front of their faces, giggling. They were all wearing high-waisted jeans and trendy crop tops that they must have coordinated beforehand.

"Makes you feel old, don't it?" Pam teased, bumping her hip up against mine.

"Nah. Just wiser," I said, adjusting my purse across my chest and settling it on my right hip. I clicked the automatic lock button on my key fob. "And it's too damn cold for tube tops anyway."

As we approached the glowing orange lights of the restaurant entrance, I immediately spotted Jerry standing out front. His hands were tucked in his jean pockets. The gaggle of pretty girls went by, but he didn't seem to notice.

Jerry had a face like a ham hock, sweaty and pink. He's definitely not what I'd call handsome, but his close-set brown eyes were kind, and his mischievous, joker-like smile was undoubtedly his most attractive feature. The three of us had been friends for nearly a decade now, working together at the same marketing firm.

For the longest time, I thought Jerry and Pam had a

"thing", but she had assured me it was never like that. If Jerry dated, Pam and I didn't know about it. He seemed perfectly content with being single.

"Happy birthday, love," Jerry scooped me into a hug, lifting my feet off the ground as he did so.

"Oh, wow. Someone's excited tonight," Pam teased.

"Thanks, Jerry," I said, adjusting my skirt as he dropped me back down on the pavement.

"I saw you this morning, remember? He already wished me a happy birthday like fifty times," I told Pam.

"Yeah, but you know how it is. Nothing at work feels real. Now we can really celebrate. The big four-oh! It's supposed to be a big one, you know..." Jerry held open the entrance door for Pam and me.

"I can't stay long," I tried to tell them, but I was hit with a blast of live music and people chattering. Trying to talk now was like screaming into a deep dark void.

Jerry pointed through the crowd at an open table near the bar, but away from the band, and Pam and I led the way.

"Wow. I can't believe this place gets so crowded. Definitely different than the lunch crowd," I shouted, taking a seat at the four-person table. I hopped up on one of the stools and tried to scoot in closer to the table. The seats were so high that my feet dangled several inches from the ground.

"So, what did you and Delaney do for your birthday? Anything?" Jerry asked, leaning in, his expression hopeful.

He was sitting across from me, Pam at his elbow. They were sitting so close to one another, and, once again, it crossed my mind that they were a couple. If not, maybe they should be...

"No, nothing. Although we wouldn't have had time to anyway." I brought him up to speed on what had happened to Samantha.

Our waitress swooped in, taking our drink order.

"Serves her right," Jerry mumbled under his breath. He adjusted the sugar packets on the table and rearranged the bottles of ketchup and steak sauce.

"Jerry don't say that," Pam slapped his arm and widened her eyes at me.

"Well, it's true. She stole Ivy's husband. You can't shit on people like that and expect karma not to rear up sooner or later..."

My mind wandered back to the day Michael had told me '*I've met someone. I think you and I both know it's for the best...*' He was no nonchalant when he said it and I instantly felt too foolish to speak the truth – that I *was* shocked. In fact, I felt completely blindsided by it.

I'd thought things were okay between us, better than okay, actually.

The waitress returned with a tray full of drinks. She placed our drinks neatly in front of us on matching coasters. An amaretto sour for me. Dark Belgian beers for Jerry and Pam.

We clinked our glasses together jovially, then I took a

long swig of mine. My cheeks puckered and I set the drink back down on the table.

"First of all, nobody *stole* Michael from me. He chose to go on his own. And although I'm not crazy about Samantha, Laney is. She likes her, and right now, Laney doesn't like much of anyone. So, I can't, in good conscience, ever wish ill of Michael's wife."

Pam and Jerry exchanged looks, clearly impressed. I must admit, I was impressed myself. I sat up straighter and took another sip of the acidic drink.

I meant what I said. I don't want anything bad to happen to Laney's stepmom. But a few years ago, that wouldn't have been the case.

"I'm proud of you. You've really turned over a new leaf, my friend." Pam reached across the table and squeezed my hand. The gesture was kind and I was surprised to feel my eyes watering uncontrollably. Jerry tapped my toe under the table and smiled. Just like that, I felt my shoulders loosen, the tension in my stomach easing.

It's my birthday. And I have two awesome friends here with me. Hell, I might be forty and I might be divorced, but I like my job and I love my friends. And most importantly, I still have Laney, even if she's going through a rebellious teenage phase...

"Speaking of new leaves, Pam and I have something to tell you," Jerry said, out of the blue.

I watched my two best friends exchange smirky little smiles again.

Were they finally going to admit that they were dating?

"Well, come on then. Spill those guts," I teased, sloshing the ice around in my drink with a straw. I could already feel a smidge of heartburn rising from my stomach.

"We sort of ... well, we did a thing. For your birthday, Ivy," Pam grimaced.

"Oh?" I said, slightly disappointed.

I'm not a fan of gifts or big displays of affection.

Jerry and Pam knew that better than anyone.

Jerry took out his shiny black Android, flashed another knowing smile at Pam, then set his phone down on the table. He clicked the home button and slid it across the table toward me.

I stared at the screen and blinked. My own face peered back at me.

"What is this?"

I recognized the picture: me, in a slim-fitting cocktail dress, cleavage propped up more than usual. Pam had taken the photo at last year's Christmas party; it was one of those rare pictures that turned out well only because I wasn't trying too hard to smile, or to get the right angle. She'd sent it to me last year, encouraging me to use it as my profile pic on Facebook. I had considered it, but ultimately, decided not to. I looked too carefree and silly in the photo.

"Scroll down." Jerry tapped his pointer finger on the table, excitedly. He looked all too pleased with himself.

A flicker of irritation rolled through me.

What the hell had they gone and done now?

I did what he said and scrolled.

Ivy, 30, from Madison, Indiana
Likes: camping trips, boating, scary movies, thriller novels

"Camping? Thriller novels? What the hell is this, guys? And you put my age down as 30! Why?" I was laughing, but my face felt hot.

My best friends set me up a dating profile! It doesn't get more pathetic than that...

"You can change it up any way you'd like. It's not live yet, so don't be mad. We just thought it'd be good for you, ya know? You're kind and funny, not to mention smoking hot ... and you deserve to have some fun," Pam gushed. She scanned my face, waiting for my approval.

"You guys suck, you know that?" I covered my face with my hands, rubbing them up and down.

"Here's the log-in information and password. You can change anything you'd like. We added some more stuff about you, too ... and there are two more pictures on there." Jerry passed me a yellow sticky note with the words IvyGirl807 and 35818 written on it in his sloppy scrawl.

I snatched the note up and jammed it inside the purse on the stool beside me.

Our waitress had reappeared, this time with a steaming white plate of mussels.

"Ooh, that's a great picture of you," she crooned, wiggling her brows at the photo displayed on Jerry's phone.

My cheeks flushed and I flipped the phone over on the table.

"Thanks," I said, quietly.

"There are so many attractive guys on there. And girls too! Promise me you'll check it out," Pam whined, slamming back her second beer and shouting after the waitress for a third.

"I will," I lied, fingers grasping one of the mussel shells. "So, how was your day off?" I tried to change the subject, uncomfortable with this intense focus on me and my lackluster love life.

I sucked the flesh from the shell while Pam told Jerry and me about her two intakes at the shelter today—an abused labrador and a lost Balinese kitten. She had been volunteering at the local animal shelter every Friday and Saturday for years now, and though she was one of those people who viewed animals as children, she never brought any home with her from work.

Oh, how nice it would be to have a sassy pup instead of a rabid teen in my house...

I was grateful to have a change in topic. I listened to my friends talk, but I didn't hear much of what they said because I was slightly irritated about the whole dating site thing.

Who the fuck do they think they are setting that up without asking me? Am I that desperate in their eyes?

I tried to imagine the conversation that must have taken place between them when they decided to set it up. Pam saying, *'Poor Ivy. You know what she really needs for her birthday? A man!'*

Pam was single too, but she dated regularly, either guys she met on dating sites or blokes she met in bars. Unlike me, she had never been married.

I was also still worried about Delaney and Samantha. I checked my phone for the hundredth time but Michael had not responded to my texts.

Surely, if Delaney needed me, she would get a hold of me, I assured myself.

"Helloooo," Jerry said, breaking into my thoughts with the snap of his fingers.

"What?" I snapped. "Sorry. Just thinking about Delaney again…"

"Well, we're trying to get your mind off that. Where should we go next? You're the birthday girl, you decide."

"Next?" I took a sip of my drink. By now, the amaretto sour was lukewarm, and the mussels were swishing around in my belly. All I wanted to do was go back home and fall asleep early.

Damn, maybe I am getting old.

"Yeah, I thought we could go out to a club. There are some new ones that just opened over in Kentucky. Maybe have some more drinks, do a little dancing like the old days? And before you say no, don't worry. Jerry will be the DD if we need him," Pam pleaded.

The words "no" and "I'm tired" floated on the tip of my tongue. And they wouldn't have been a lie – I was tired. And stressed out.

I want to go home, crawl into bed, and sleep.

But my mind wandered back to the dating profile, that giddy, carefree version of me in that profile pic. And my friends, so desperate to see me dating again. Maybe it wasn't a terrible idea, but it still made me nervous just thinking about it. The last man I was with was Michael, and ... well, look how that turned out.

"Okay, I'll go ... but only for a little while. I need to get home in case—"

"We know, we know. In case Delaney needs you," Jerry said, laughing.

Pam and Jerry were kind enough to settle the bill, covering my part of the food and my drink for my birthday. As we walked outside, I was hit with a vague memory: stumbling out of a restaurant just like this one...only then, it had been my twenty-first birthday. Michael clutching my arm for support. We were both drunk, completely unfit to be driving. But we didn't care – we were so in love, or lust, that all we could think about was getting back to his apartment, getting each other alone...

'I can't wait to get you back to my place. Give you some birthday dessert, baby,' he'd purred in my ear. He flicked my lobe with his tongue. It was cheesy – all of it – but his words created tingly shocks of pleasure that started on my scalp and trickled all the way to my toes.

Michael, always the charmer. Until he wasn't.

"Listen, I'm going to follow you there," I said, opening the door of the van. I expected more protests and was relieved when they didn't.

It had been so long since I'd been to Grisham Boulevard, which was where most of the popular bars and night clubs were in Kentucky.

"You sure you don't want to ride with me now? You could leave your car here till morning," Jerry stood outside the driver's window, jingling his keys. Pam was clutching his arm, clearly too drunk to drive herself after those four beers.

"Nah, that's okay. I'll park in the garage by Grisham, and then if I need you to take me home, at least I'll know the van is safely parked."

In reality, I wasn't planning on having any more drinks. The amaretto sour had hurt my belly and left a terrible aftertaste in the back of my mouth.

Plus, I wanted to be able to drive home so I didn't have to deal with tracking down my van in the morning. Too many days in my youth had been spent recuperating from the night before...

I placed my purse on the passenger seat and tugged my driver's mirror down to check for food in my teeth.

Even now, I'm shocked by the woman looking back at me.

I guess I was still expecting that younger version, the one with the smooth white skin and shiny black hair minus the wiry gray strands, the girl with the killer smile and the confidence to back it up. Once upon a time, I could turn heads. Including Michael's.

But I don't turn heads anymore.

Maybe the dating app isn't such a bad idea, I considered.

Pam had shared a few stories about her dating escapades with me. Was I impressed?

No, not really. I sort of felt sorry for her.

My mind drifted back to Delaney, as I waited for Jerry to pull up beside me so I could follow him there.

The phone on the floorboard chirped again. I'd nearly forgotten about it, lying down there in the dark. Grunting, I reached across the seat and scooped it up.

Delaney will definitely be wanting this back in the morning, I thought, furtively.

I stared at the screen of her iPhone. The screen saver was a picture of her and her best friend, Kerry. Kerry was all smiles and puckered lips, but Delaney … she frowned into the lens, her eyes narrowed and intense. She looked almost … *angry.* And everything about the photo screamed: '*Don't fuck with me.*'

Maybe that's exactly what she was aiming for, I considered.

I swiped right, mostly to erase that vexed image of her, and was instantly met with a prompt to put in a password. Without thinking I punched in the six-digit code Delaney and I had both been using for years now, the one she used to use for Roblox and other online kid games. But that had been years ago; surely, she had changed it by now?

Surprisingly, the password still worked. Like me, Delaney was a creature of habit.

A dozen app icons filled the screen. I was relieved to see

311

that her wallpaper was a simple design, blue ocean water and steamy white caps on a stranded beach. It felt wrong looking at her phone like this. And if Delaney knew I was snooping, there would be hell to pay.

She would be livid, no doubt.

But isn't this what responsible parents are supposed to do? Check up on their teens?

My mother was dead by the time I was Delaney's age, and I could have used one with all the trouble I got into.

Delaney had two unread text messages blinking back at me in the corner. Before I could change my mind, I clicked on the message app.

The first one was the message I'd sent her earlier, telling her to call me if she needed me.

And the newest one... I clicked on it and waited for an image to load on the screen.

My mouth fell open and I released a small cry, covering my mouth in horror.

"What're ya doing over there? Let's go!" Pam shouted from Jerry's passenger window. They were parked right in front of me, blinding white headlights shining in my eyes.

I quickly pressed the home button and the screen went dark. Shaking, I reached over for my purse and buried the phone deep inside.

I rolled my window all the way down, leaned out, then shouted, "I'm so sorry, but I have to go now. Delaney needs me at the hospital. Thanks for dinner. We'll do it again soon, yeah?"

"Yeah, of course," Pam said, but I could tell she didn't believe me. She slumped back in her seat, and I could see she was already texting away on her phone.

If Jerry and I are here, then who is she texting? I wondered.

Pam didn't have any other close friends, but she was friendly with a lot of people…

But it didn't matter – my thoughts were with Delaney now.

The image on my daughter's phone flashed in my mind again. Repulsed, I shook my head, willing it to go away. Jerry honked and waved, then I watched their taillights disappear from the restaurant parking lot. Finally, I put the van in gear and started the slow crawl home.

The One Night Stand: Chapter 4

BEFORE

The house was cloaked in a dark cloud, not a single light on inside or outside, since I'd left them all off when I'd gone out for my birthday.

Oak Hill was not only a subdivision, but a *community*. At least that was what the original advertisement had claimed. I had one neighbor across the street; both houses beside me – near replicas of mine – lay neglected and empty.

Almost all the houses in Oak Hill were empty. The clubhouse and the pool that they boasted about building years ago ... well, those never happened. The people and the houses in the brochure were sunshiny, gleaming with community, with joy and a stark contrast to the somber reality I came home to every day.

A perfect house in theory; but a lonely, empty place in truth.

It was like living in our own little ghost town, which at first, when we moved in, we thought was neat. I never had to worry about Delaney riding her bike outside, but then again, there was no one for her to play with either. And as the years marched on, the whole subdivision felt deserted and a little depressing.

At least we have Fran across the street, I thought, rolling my eyes.

Fran looked to be around seventy years old and, according to Pam's sources, she was widowed. Although she rarely left the house, she was always watching, peeking through the blinds as we came or went, goggling at us when she fetched her mail. And although I'd tried being neighborly, waving and smiling, she was never friendly back, almost pretending like she didn't see us at all.

Finally, after the first year of living here, I stopped waving completely.

Maybe she's senile, I had considered. *Or maybe her vision's gone bad.*

Or maybe she doesn't like having neighbors, period.

Tonight, her house was as dark as ours, giving the entire neighborhood the hush of an overgrown, forgotten cemetery. The empty houses were like looming headstones, a reminder of what could have been.

I wonder where Fran is. She's usually home, every night...

Hell, maybe Fran is out on a date. I wouldn't be surprised if her love life was better than mine, I thought, glumly.

I locked the van, then followed the stony pathway up to my front door. I let myself in, clicking the door locked behind me and slammed into something tall and hard, yelping in pain.

"Damn you!" I kicked the vacuum cleaner on its side, then stopped myself and took a breath.

It's going to be okay. Just stay calm, Ivy.

Room by room I went, flooding the house with lights. The house came alive, instantly making me feel better, and more in control. I imagined how it would look from space, one glowing bulb in the center of a pitch-black ghost land.

I shimmied out of my pencil skirt and too-tight blouse, then tugged on my favorite sweats and a raggedy old Bengals t-shirt.

I hardly ever drank, but that amaretto had got me going, so I tracked down an old bottle of Moscato in the back of the fridge, then slid out a dusty old wine glass from the cupboard.

I blew the dust off and poured, sighing as I did so.

What am I going to do with that daughter of mine?

The image on her phone came rushing back…

I tipped the glass back, eager to taste the sweet cherry fizz.

I swallowed, slowly, then squinted into the glass.

What the hell?

Just to be sure, I took a few more sips.

Yep. No doubt. This is water, not wine.

So, Laney was drinking. Enough to know that she had to cover her tracks by switching out the nearly forgotten bottle in the back of the fridge. Add that to my growing list of concerns.

I turned the bottle on its side over the sink basin, watching as the long, slow stream chugged down the drain in splashy waves.

Laney is drinking. But that is small potatoes compared to what I found on her phone.

Angrily, I launched the bottle across the room. It landed with a hard clank on the floor beside the trash, but it didn't break.

Go figure.

I only tear up things I want to fix. Never the other way around anymore.

I stomped towards my daughter's room. Her door was closed, which wasn't unusual. Delaney was all about her privacy these days.

Finally, I understand why.

Weekends were the only time I was home alone in the house. I'd considered snooping in the past, but there was something about it that always made me uneasy, guilty, for not allowing her this one safe space she could call her own.

And how would I feel if she was snooping through my room?

But in reality, how smart is it to give her so much space and privacy?

I wasn't sure anymore.

Not very smart, apparently.

The light was off in her room. I flipped it on, giving my eyes a few seconds to adjust. I rarely saw the place anymore. Delaney slipped in and out like a phantom – a flash in the morning, a blip at the dinner table, a quiet little mouse at bedtime...

It had been so long since I'd been in her room that I'd nearly forgotten what it looked like.

I was surprised to find it neat and organized. The bed was made; the same fuzzy blue blanket with little curls of lace was tucked stiffly in each corner.

Bob, the stuffed elephant, was perched in the center of her pillows.

My heart swelled at the sight of him. I sank down on the bed, the springs squeaky and old, and I reached for the frumpy old toy. His short gray hair was coarser than I remembered – it used to feel so soft and smooth on my fingertips. I could remember packing Bob in the car and in her night bag on trips to Michael's, because Delaney couldn't go without him.

Now, his fur felt stiff and matted. He'd gotten old. Just like me. Just like Delaney... She's not a smooth little girl anymore; she's coarser, rougher around the edges...

She's keeping a secret.

I took her phone out of my pocket and clicked the home screen. Taking a deep breath, I clicked on the messages again. It felt wrong – so damn wrong – looking at this image.

It was a picture of a naked boy.

A boy, or was it a man?

It was impossible to know for sure because his head and neck were missing. Only the space between his chest and thighs was exposed.

He gripped his penis in his hand, crudely.

It was hard to discern his age; he had some hair on his chest and the rest of his body, but there was really no way to tell. Was this a teenage boy my daughter hadn't told me about? Or was this someone else ... a predator? A stranger?

My mom brain was spinning out of control...

Luckily, from what I could tell, Delaney hadn't sent any of her own pictures.

But who knew what she had erased?

If she is sending pictures of herself, oh my God... What if this boy became angry and shared naked pictures of her all over school? Or worse, all over the internet?

There were no words exchanged, only the one picture. And it came from a number without a name, someone she didn't keep in her address book.

No name, no face, his identity a complete mystery.

I scanned through the rest of Delaney's messages, the guilt I'd felt earlier temporarily forgotten.

I saw messages from Michael and a few from Samantha. Messages from me. But other than that, there were no messages from her school friends.

Has she erased some of them? She must have, I decided.

The internet history on her cell phone showed no results.

I wasn't so old that I didn't understand what this meant: Delaney had either deleted her search history, or she was using in-private browsing.

No photos either – possibly stored on iCloud? I considered.

Besides the photo messages from the mystery man/boy, there was nothing suspect on her phone. I shut it off and stood up, placing it face down on her dresser.

Her dresser was neat, brushes and combs lined up evenly. An open makeup bag in the middle. I picked through it, fingers brushing over the new reddish-brown shadow I'd seen on her earlier. My heart ached.

I want my daughter back.

I stared at my own face in the mirror. My black hair was turning gray; the wrinkles on my forehead and between my brows were deepening by the day.

Worries like these probably don't help with wrinkles either.

I imagined Delaney standing in this exact same spot, staring at herself every day in the mirror. She was beautiful, in that way that's almost grotesque. Too perfect. Too unflawed. But she'd lost weight.

Was she self-conscious? Was she hurting more than I realized?

Monstrous beauty can seem like a blessing, but it's also a curse. Sometimes the monsters don't know how powerful their beauty is…

So, what if she's exchanging sexy pics with a boy? Is this really as big a deal as I think it is?

Wasn't I doing the exact same thing at her age? I considered.

No, I wasn't. Not because I wouldn't have, but because I was so busy grieving the loss of my parents after their car accident, and the drama I dealt with in school...

I mean, I have to talk to her about the pictures. And the alcohol. There's no question about that.

I couldn't brush it under the rug and pretend I didn't know.

I had to make sure she was at least using protection if she was considering sex...

What if she's already had sex? I shuddered at the thought of it.

But what could I do about it if she was?

She's not a child anymore.

I couldn't take her phone away – she needed it for safety.

I looked around the sweet, childlike room. It was in stark contrast to the girl who had that racy photo on her phone.

But love makes you do crazy things.

If anyone could understand that, it was me.

If Michael had asked me to send him nudes back in the day, would I have sent them?

I thought about the tickle of his words on my ear, the feathery kisses and the watery smiles and his rough fingers massaging my breasts...

Yes, I would have.

Because when you're crazy about someone, you'll do almost anything, consequences be damned.

I opened and closed Delaney's dresser drawers. I sifted through tangles of clothes in her closet.

There was nothing – no pot, no pills, no whips or chains, no deadly secrets hiding between the sheets or inside the drawers.

Just a picture of a boy, that's all.

I can handle that. After all, there are worse things a teen can do.

I had to talk to her.

Talk, not lecture, I decided. I wanted her to be able to open up to me. I never had that in a mother – a person to confide in – and I craved to be that person for Delaney. The person who made her feel safe, the person she could talk to and trust.

But does anyone trust their parents at this age? I don't know … it's hard to say when I've never experienced it…

I turned her lights back out and tightly wedged her door shut.

Somewhere in the house, I could hear my own cell phone ringing.

I ran for it, digging through my purse, desperately.

"Laney, baby?" I answered, breathily.

"Mom…" She sounded like my little girl again.

"How's Sam? Is she okay?" I closed my eyes, saying another silent prayer despite my ignorance on all things prayer related.

"She's going to be alright, I think. But her neck is broken. It could have been so much worse, Mom. She was *this* close to damaging her windpipe. And of course, if she'd damaged her spine…" I could imagine Laney on the other end, nibbling her lip and the flesh of her inner cheek.

I wish I could be there to soothe her.

"That sounds awful, but, like you said, it could have been so much worse. That must have been so scary for you and your dad."

"And the twins … they're too young to understand, and Dad is going to need my help with them, and a babysitter, until she heals."

The twins.

Something I would never get used to hearing. Unlike me, Samantha had given birth to two happy, healthy twin boys.

"Will she have to have surgery?" I asked, sitting on the edge of my bed. Unlike Delaney's bed, mine was unmade – a twisted tangle of sheets perched in the middle like a blobby white ghost.

"No. But she will have to wear a brace for several weeks and possibly do physical therapy."

"Sounds like a long road ahead. Is there anything I can do for you all? Any way I can help?"

I expected Delaney to snap at me like she'd done earlier, but she simply replied, "Thanks for offering, but I can't think of anything. We're going to stay the night here. They set us up with some cots and a play pen for the boys. Hopefully, she'll get released tomorrow or Sunday."

"Do they know what happened? Who crashed into her?"

Madison was a small town; most of us knew each other or knew *of* each other.

Delaney was quiet on the other end for several seconds.

"You still there, sweetheart?"

"Yeah, sorry. Got distracted. Honestly, I don't know who it was."

"Well, no worries. I was just being nosy. I'm relieved to hear she's okay," I said, and I meant it. I wanted my daughter to be happy, even if that meant she enjoyed spending time with another motherly figure that wasn't me.

"Happy birthday, Mom," Delaney said, catching me off guard. "I'm sorry I didn't tell you earlier. I guess ... I don't know ... I'm just stubborn sometimes. And I should have said it earlier, but then this happened and ... I forgot. I love you and I'm sorry I'm not home to celebrate with you. Remember those cakes we used to make?"

I pinched my eyes shut, fighting back tears.

"Yes, of course I do," I said, unable to hide the shake in my voice. "I miss doing that." Tears tickled the corner of each eye. It felt so good to hear my daughter, my Delaney, again.

"I wish you were here, too, but your dad and Sam and your brothers need you now. We'll have our cakes later."

"Love you," Delaney said again. I thought about the picture on her phone, the inevitable conversation we'd have to have when she got home...

But for now, I just wanted to enjoy my daughter not hating me.

"I love you too, Laney Bug. I'll talk to you tomorrow."

I clicked end and clutched the phone to my chest. Finally, I could let the tears spill over, but then my phone buzzed, vibrating against chest.

This time it was Pam.

Don't forget to check out the dating site! I want all the deets when you do!

I groaned. The irritation I'd felt earlier fluttered back, but then instantly dissipated. Maybe it was the high from Delaney's call or the traces of liquor...but, for the first time, I wondered if joining the site might be fun.

It couldn't hurt, could it?

And I'm sure they had good intentions when they set me up a profile on the site.

Michael had moved on with his new family. And Delaney ... Delaney was getting older and developing love interests of her own.

Apparently.

I have to start dating again some time. Maybe there's no better time than now.

Inside my purse, I found the crumpled piece of paper with the username and password on it.

Should I?

I could imagine Pam beside me saying, *'Hell yes, you silly bitch. Do it!'*

Delaney had swiped the wine, but she didn't know

about the stash in my bedroom. I unlocked the tiny metal safe in my closet. Beside the handgun and cash, there were two miniature bottles of whiskey. I grabbed a cold Coke and tumbler from the kitchen, then sat down at the computer with my drink. Nervously, I added the whiskey and logged onto the site.

After a few long swigs, I mustered up enough courage to click "publish" on my new dating profile.

What's the worst that could happen?

The One Night Stand: Chapter 5

NOW

What's the worst that could happen?

Well, I'll tell you what. Dead bodies. Two of them. And not a clue what to do with either.

At the kitchen table, I gripped my glass of whiskey, swishing it round and around in my hands. This time, there was no Coke. Just me and the glass and the whiskey.

Although a stiff drink was highly needed now, it wasn't a good idea – I had several tasks to complete, and one involved driving.

The dead man's car was still parked outside. I couldn't see it from the kitchen in the dark, but I could feel it there – a warning pulse, sending shivers up and down my spine.

I must get rid of that car.

For once, I was glad that Delaney was staying the night with Michael.

Which means I have all night to fix things.

I still hadn't located the man's ID, but I'd found the keys to his sleek ride tucked inside the visor. The registration and insurance in the glove box identified him as Robin Regal, a name that meant absolutely nothing to me.

But there was an address—and that itself was slightly familiar. Robin Regal lived on Grant Street, in what I guessed was an apartment in the business district of Madison.

I know his name now, but who is he exactly?

I'd never been to his house, but I knew the area.

How did he get here, and why did he come?

I'd gone on several dates over the last few weeks, but not with this man, and not with anyone from my own town of Madison.

He wasn't a friend of Michael's, not someone I knew from work.

There was nothing to connect us.

Nothing except for the fact that his body's here and his car is sitting out front.

If it was just him, maybe I would have called the cops, but the other body. That was the one that really troubled me.

That is the one I'm responsible for, I know it.

I peeked through the side of the blinds. My neighbor

Fran usually went to bed around nine or ten which meant I had about an hour to make plans.

It had been years since I'd gone down to the grimy old cellar underneath our house. But slowly, I descended the steps, the slaps of my bare feet echoing grimly in the hollow space. Using the flashlight app on my phone, I shone it around in the dark. The dank space smelled earthy and was filthier than I remembered. Cobwebs clung to the corners, glistening eerily in the dark, and my heart skipped a beat as a cockroach scuttled across my bare foot.

I held the phone out, looking for more creepy crawlies. I had no doubt they were there, those beady eyes and fat, bulging bodies hiding in the rafters, watching me from the musty black corners of the room...

My light hovered over three black shapes in the corner.

Three long bags were propped against the wall – Michael's old golf bags. There was a time when he just *had* to have them, but just like his interest in me, his obsession with golfing waned, then fizzled out completely. Now I was stuck with his clubs, taking up space, collecting dust in every crevice of my life...

One by one, I laid the clunky, black bags on their sides, and started unloading the clubs. They clanked on the concrete floor, hopefully scaring away any nearby critters.

When all three bags were empty, I tugged them up the stairs, one by one. Even empty, the thick, glossy leather was heavy. Back in my room, I laid the bags on the floor beside the bodies.

What seemed like a good idea at first now seemed silly. Each bag was over five feet, Robin Regal was nearly six.

This isn't going to work.

Nice plan, Ivy.

My face paled, my stomach twisting in knots, as the realization kicked in: if I wanted to fit the bodies into the bags, I'd have to cut them into pieces to do it.

Get your copy of *The One Night Stand* today to find out what happens next...

YOUR NUMBER ONE STOP

ONE MORE CHAPTER

FOR PAGETURNING BOOKS

One More Chapter is an
award-winning global
division of HarperCollins.

Sign up to our newsletter to get our
latest eBook deals and stay up to date
with our weekly Book Club!
<u>Subscribe here.</u>

Meet the team at
<u>www.onemorechapter.com</u>

Follow us!
 @OneMoreChapter_
 @OneMoreChapter
 @onemorechapterhc

Do you write unputdownable fiction?
We love to hear from new voices.
Find out how to submit your novel at
<u>www.onemorechapter.com/submissions</u>